The Answer

Even the book morphs!
Flip the pages
and check it out!

Look for other **ANIMORPHS**®
titles by K.A. Applegate:

The Answer

K.A. Applegate

AN
APPLE
PAPERBACK

SCHOLASTIC INC.
New York Toronto London Auckland Sydney
Mexico City New Delhi Hong Kong

Cover illustration by David B. Mattingly
Art Direction/Design by Karen Hudson/Ursula Albano

ISBN 0-439-11527-2

12 11 10 9 8 7 6 5 4 3   1 2 3 4 5 6/0

Printed in the U.S.A.
First Scholastic printing, May 2001

For Scott Bremner

And for Michael and Jake

The Answer

CHAPTER 1

<They're going after the elementary school,> Tobias said.

<They're going after everything,> I answered.

<Why are they doing this? It makes no sense,> Tobias said. <It's not just brutal; it's stupid. Pointless destruction.>

The nearest Bug fighter swooped low and slow. It fired its Dracon beams and the two-story gym exploded into charred stucco and twisted steel beams.

It drifted almost casually above the tired old low-slung classrooms and fired again, dragging the beam end-to-end along the buildings.

<They're sending a message,> I said. <Mess with us and this is what we do.>

We had destroyed the Yeerk pool. The Yeerk pool was now the world's biggest sinkhole. It looked like a crater. It was a crater, with half the mall in ruins on one slope, jumbled bits of fast-food restaurants, streetlights, ripped up concrete, cars, skinny trees, all tumbled together at the bottom. The water of the Yeerk pool, looking like molten lead, soaked up through the dirt. An Exxon sign lay half-submerged in it. A couple of dozen empty one-liter soda bottles drifted around like someone's idea of toy boats.

How many Yeerks had died? Certainly thousands. Maybe tens of thousands. How many Hork-Bajir? How many Taxxons?

Humans?

We had tried to warn people, but the devastation had been too complete, had come too suddenly.

<It's not a message, Big Jake,> Marco said. <The Yeerks know now that we'll do whatever we have to do, they know it's all-out war. We blew up their only on-planet food supply. We're way past sending messages. Look: They're drawing a circle.>

Marco was a hundred feet higher up than me. He was in osprey morph, I was in falcon, Tobias was himself: a red-tailed hawk.

<Marco's right,> Tobias said. <They're making a big circle.>

More Bug fighters than I'd ever seen in one place. Maybe fifty of the things. They blasted schools; they blasted businesses; they blasted homes and churches. The shock waves would reach us, echoes of destruction. Pillars of smoke rose high in the air. Fires, some blazing and roaring, others smoldering sullenly, created thermal updrafts that were bread and butter to three mismatched birds of prey. We soared easily, effortlessly. We had the best possible seats for the show. With raptor eyes we could see every sickening detail. We could not miss a shot, could not fail to see lovingly tended gardens, prized homes, businesses, cars, burn as quickly and brightly as match heads.

The refugees — people who had been our neighbors, friends, classmates — the shocked, scared, lost refugees fled on foot, carrying what they could, running between stalled cars. Overpasses were all down, traffic lights all off, bridges were collapsed: Nothing with four wheels was moving.

A news helicopter was perhaps five miles off, no doubt filming and sending the pictures out live. The Yeerks could easily shoot down the copter. They were letting it film. Maybe even piloting the craft themselves. They wanted the world to see the violence. They wanted humans

3

to be afraid. The infiltration phase of the war was over, over. From now on the Yeerks would be as subtle as sledgehammers.

I caught a rush of warm air, the thermal energy released by a burning supermarket, and I soared higher, up and up. I could see what Marco and Tobias had understood: The Yeerks were creating a circle of annihilation. The collapsed Yeerk pool was the center. They were burning, blackening everything in a radius of two miles.

That would be virtually all of what had been our home town.

And I had done it. I had given the order to destroy the Yeerk pool. All of this was a result.

But why? That was what bothered me. This wasn't the time for moaning over the destruction, or even for second-guessing myself. I was done with that. Why? Why were the Yeerks doing this?

<Maybe they think we're down there,> Tobias suggested.

I noticed something in the far distance, south of where we were. More smoke. And with my falcon's eyes I could just barely make out hints of still more Bug fighters. They looked like a cloud of gnats.

Tobias yelled. <Hey! Jets!>

I followed the direction of his gaze, and sure enough, there they were: a flight of four F-16's.

They were racing straight toward us. Straight toward the Bug fighters.

<It's suicide,> Marco said.

We watched, helpless to do anything. We had spent the morning watching helplessly.

The F-16's came straight in. Two of the Bug fighters broke off from torching civilian buildings and turned lazily to meet the attack.

Missiles flew from the F-16's and the jets broke away. Two Dracon beams fired and the missiles were destroyed in midflight.

The Bug fighters accelerated, easily caught the jets, and fired again. Three of the four exploded. There were no parachutes. No possibility of parachutes. The fourth jet rocketed low, leveled off seeming inches from the scorched ground and hit afterburners.

The Bug fighters let him go: They had nothing to fear.

No, that wasn't quite true. The Yeerks were scared, just not of jets. This circle of destruction was evidence of fear. They were creating a barrier of sorts: not a wall, but a desert of ash and cinder so that an enemy wouldn't be able to get close, unseen.

It gave me a grim satisfaction. The Yeerks were scared of us. But what were they protecting? The ruins of the Yeerk pool?

5

<The helicopter!> Marco yelled.

The Yeerks had decided that show time was over. They torched the news copter. A twirling cinder fell to Earth.

<Something's going to happen,> I said.

<And there it is,> Tobias said, as always more observant in the air than any of us.

It was as big as a sports arena. It moved slowly, cumbersome in atmosphere. It was designed for space, not, like the Bug fighters, to be comfortable in air.

The Pool ship looked like a fat, swollen, three-legged spider. I'd seen it before, up in orbit, high above planet Earth.

The Pool ship: home of the Yeerk invasion force, base of the Bug fighters. It was a space-going Yeerk pool, well-defended, dangerous, but essentially a portable barracks, a giant mess hall that served up hearty doses of Kandrona rays, the sustenance that a Yeerk must have every three days or die.

The Bug fighters rose to greet their mother, swarming around the Pool ship, bristling, daring anyone to attack.

The Pool ship waddled down out of the sky, shouldering through the clouds. And gently, delicately, ever-so-tentatively, it rested its bulk on terra firma.

<The Pool ship,> Marco whispered reverently. <The mother of all targets. I would give both of my arms to see that thing burn.> Then he laughed harshly. <You know what this means, don't you?>

<They're getting hungry,> I said. <They're getting *very* hungry.>

CHAPTER 2

My name is Jake.

My name is Jake Berenson. The days of secrecy, of lurking in the shadows are over. The Yeerks know my name. They know my height, weight, eye color, Social Security number, and favorite foods. At long last they know the word *Animorph,* Marco's word for us.

My brother Tom is one of them, a human-Controller. He has been for a long time. He's been elevated to security chief for all Yeerk forces on Earth.

My parents, my mom and dad, are Controllers now, too. Host bodies for Yeerks.

They know it all now, the Yeerks do. All our names. All our deeds.

I've fought them for more than three years. I was just thirteen when I started. I'm sixteen now, though that fact, like so many facts, has been deliberately obscured in the secret accounts we've kept.

I'm a sixteen-year-old kid named Jake Berenson, and I am the leader of the Animorphs.

In the past it's been hard for me to say that, to take on the title of leader. In the past I've questioned myself. Wondered whether I was right, wondered whether what I did was good, wondered whether I had any right to make life-and-death decisions. I've felt sorry for myself at times. Maybe anyone would, in my spot.

But I had to put all that aside now. I had put it *all* aside. Not because I was suddenly convinced that I deserved the power, was worthy of it. That wasn't it. I knew better than to get too caught up in the myth of Mighty Jake the Yeerk Killer.

I had given up soul-searching because I realized now that it was simply too late. Way past too late. The battle had become a war. And I was, for better or worse, the only leader we had.

From here on out the second-guessing, the legitimate doubts, and the self-indulgent whining, they were over. Save them for my old age in the unlikely event that I ever had an old age.

We were all still alive, Cassie, Marco, Rachel,

9

Tobias, and me. We'd been formed into a group by accident. A chance encounter in an abandoned construction site with a dying Andalite prince named Elfangor. He had given the five of us the Andalite power to morph, to become any animal we could touch. Later Elfangor's brother Ax had joined us.

We were just kids. But in some ways we were the ideal guerrilla fighters. The morphing power let us fly and dig and crawl, sense, hide, and fight with far more than human power. Our youth made us the least likely of suspects.

The Yeerks had carried on a subversive war of infiltration for more than a decade. They had first discovered our planet back at the time of the Gulf War. For various reasons their then Visser One had fashioned a plan to slowly infiltrate human society, infest hundreds, then thousands, eventually millions of humans with the Yeerk parasite, and when it was too late to stop them, seize sudden control of the planet. Only then would the Yeerks finalize an almost bloodless conquest.

But that visser moved on and was replaced in command of Earth by the evil creature we had long known as Visser Three. Visser Three was a less subtle enemy. Less adept at subversion. A brute. We had fought him, lost, won, but above all survived. And, in surviving, we had slowed his conquest, frustrated his plans, driven him to ever wilder schemes. We had forced his hand, in the end, I guess.

Now the war of subversion was over. Visser Three was promoted to Visser One and all his most brutal instincts were unleashed.

In this new, open war, we had scored some impressive victories. We had destroyed the Yeerk pool. And we helped to motivate at least partial and spotty efforts by the military to respond to the Yeerk threat. Marco's mom was free of her Yeerk slave master, free of the violent, dangerous creature who had been the very Yeerk who launched the invasion of Earth — Visser One. That Visser One was dead and his human host now worked with us. We had used the morphing cube to make new Animorphs, to increase our numbers.

But we had taken hits, too: We had all been driven from our homes. We had lost all vestiges of a normal life. We now hid with the free Hork-Bajir in a valley deep in the mountains.

And we had lost the morphing cube. The Yeerks had it. My brother Tom had taken it, and, when I might have stopped him — Cassie had let him and it go.

With that act, Cassie had surrendered our edge, our one great advantage: that we alone had the power to morph.

The Andalite technology was now in Yeerk

hands, and we had already seen that Yeerks were using it just as we had used it: to capture all the amazing powers to be found in the animal kingdom.

The six of us, Marco, Rachel, Tobias, Ax, Cassie, and I, had stayed together through impossibly bad times, through every defeat, every close call, every mind-twisting weirdness, every horror. None of us had ever turned against the others. There had never been a betrayal.

Cassie let Tom take the morphing cube. Perhaps she had done so because to her the alternative was worse: She feared for me, for my soul I guess, if I was forced to kill my own brother.

Not good enough. Not for me. All that counted now was that we win, and Cassie, maybe for the most decent of motives, had hurt us badly.

I loved Cassie. Always had. Still did. But there was this thing between us now. And I could never trust her again. She had put my personal well-being ahead of winning a war we *absolutely* could not lose. And, I knew, that her decision might have come in part from my own self-doubts, my own inability to throw off moral ambiguity.

If I had been stronger . . . if I had been as strong as I should be, maybe Cassie would not have made her fatal mistake. I saw that clearly now. Too late for either of us.

And that was the other reason why I would allow myself no more second-guessing. A leader who shows weakness invites disaster.

We flew back to the Hork-Bajir camp. And as we flew I thought. Not about how my orders to destroy the Yeerk pool had resulted in the literal obliteration of the city, but about how, how, how I could destroy the Pool ship.

And about that distant pillar of smoke away to the south.

There had to be a way to take out the Pool ship. Destroy that ship and the war might be won. It was the target I could not possibly resist.

A fact that would be known by my brother Tom, and my parents, and by their ruler, Visser One.

13

CHAPTER 3

"It's too dangerous." That was Eva, Marco's mom. The woman who had been host body to the first Visser One. "Visser One will know that you know. He'll know you're coming. He can't let you destroy a Pool ship — that's the only large-scale food supply the Yeerks have. The Blade ship can only service so many. Lose a Pool ship? The Council of Thirteen would have Visser One executed."

Marco shook his head. "He'll think we're cocky after taking out the Yeerk pool. Maybe he'll underestimate us."

"No," Eva said flatly. "He'll never underestimate you again. That's over."

14

We stood around a small fire. It was chilly. Fog had a tendency to form in this deep valley, sometimes so thick we could barely see our hands in front of our faces. It wasn't that bad now, but it was still cold.

"It's too dangerous," Cassie's dad said. He was sipping a cup of what passed for coffee here in our rough-and-ready camp.

"This is a job for the military now," Rachel's mom argued. "You kids have done enough. The secret is out: Leave it to the people who should be protecting this country. I mean, we paid enough in taxes to support the military; well, now let's see what we got for all that money."

We were in a council of war. I was getting so I hated these meetings. Too many voices, too many opinions. So many opinions sometimes that it seemed the consensus would always come down on the side of doing nothing.

But we were guests among the free Hork-Bajir. This was their valley, their trees, the only home they had. We'd come running to them with our families in tow when we needed a place to hide. So at the very least I had to listen to Toby, the young female Hork-Bajir seer. And only a fool would dismiss Eva's input: None of us knew the Yeerks half as well. And of course, there were my fellow Animorphs.

But added to all that we had Marco's dad; Rachel's mom; James, the representative of our new, adjunct Animorphs; Tobias's mom; both of Cassie's parents, who only cared about making sure no one got hurt . . . too many people with too many agendas. But I still didn't know how to tell adults, my friends' parents no less, to be quiet and let me do my job.

I tried not to show my impatience, but these days I'm not so good at that. Cassie was watching me. We're not as close anymore, but she still knows me.

She said, "Look folks, we're going to try. I don't think the question is really 'whether' but 'how.'"

"No one has decided any such thing," Rachel's mom said angrily. "My daughter is not going to be dragged into some suicidal undertaking like this."

Rachel laughed. Rachel's not a person who'll be one way with her friends and another way with her family. There's only one version of Rachel. "Mom, if we go, I go. If we don't go, I still go. Visser One parks his Pool ship right out in the open and we're not going to ram it down his nonexistent throat? Hah! I'm with Marco: Blow it up. Blow it up real good."

I hid a grin. Rachel is the original Nike girl:

Just do it. Just do it, and if that doesn't work do it harder and meaner.

"It seems a waste to simply blow it up," Toby said, speaking for the first time. The Hork-Bajir are a fearsome-looking, but basically peaceful race that, left alone, would live in the trees eating bark and caring for the forest. Toby is one of a rare Hork-Bajir mutation: a seer. A sort of Hork-Bajir intellectual and leader. She leads the free Hork-Bajir, a small but growing band of Hork-Bajir who have been liberated from their parasitic masters.

"What do you mean?" I asked Toby.

"There are hundreds of captive Hork-Bajir aboard the Pool ship," Toby said. "If we could free at least a portion of them . . . and of course there are the ship's massive weapons systems. Imagine controlling all that power."

"Take it?" Marco yelped. "*Steal* the Pool ship!"

Rachel jabbed a finger at Toby. "This is my girl," she said.

Rachel's "girl" was nearly six and a half feet tall, and looked an awful lot like a kid's notion of a goblin. Not to mention the fact that she was armed with razor-sharp blades growing from wrists and elbows and forehead.

<It is the approach Visser One would not expect,> Ax opined cautiously. <It is, of course, im-

17

possible. It is not like stealing a Bug fighter. Every system on board the Pool ship is encrypted, and the codes will probably change hourly. It might take me an hour to break any one sequence, and if I am a minute late it will roll over and I will be starting back at the beginning. An hour to get you into navigation, for example, if I am lucky. And another hour to gain access to weapons systems.>

And then everyone started talking at once, arguing, posturing, scoring debating points.

"Okay," I said holding up my hands for calm. "That's enough, folks, thanks for coming."

"You don't just dismiss us!" Rachel's mom yelled.

"Sure he does, Mom," Rachel said cheerfully.

"I need Rachel, Marco, Tobias, Ax, Toby, James, and Eva," I said.

I hadn't meant to exclude Cassie. I really hadn't. But it was too late. She looked like I'd hit her. She blinked and turned quickly away, covering the moment with aimless chatter to her parents.

Tobias gave me a dirty look. And if you think a red-tailed hawk's gaze is always a dirty look, you're close to being right. Still, I knew Tobias was mad at me. Everyone was. Everyone but James who was excited to be included, and Eva who hadn't really caught what was going on with me and Cassie.

There was nothing to be done now. I couldn't go running after Cassie. The insult had been delivered. There was no taking it back now.

I said, "As much as I hate to admit it, Rachel's mom is partly right: This isn't just our fight anymore. Three pilots died today. Probably Air National Guard. It shows that there are military forces out there that could help."

"All due respect," Marco said, "those pilots didn't do much good."

"If we're going after the Pool ship we need a diversion," I said. "We'll need a great big diversion. I want tanks and jets and soldiers. And I want us — some of us at least — to be right out there in front with them. I want Visser One to be dead sure we're trying to either blow up his precious ship or get inside it."

"And we will be, right?" James asked. "I mean, one or the other, right?"

I shook my head. "Visser One will consider the possibility that we're using the attack as a cover. He's slow but he's not a complete idiot. He'll figure one of three things: First, the attack is the real thing. Second, the attack is a cover for the next attack. Third, the attack is a cover for us to infiltrate the ship and destroy it from inside. Any of those three options he does the same thing: lifts the ship off and amuses himself blasting everything in sight with the Pool ship's big Dracon cannon."

"Okay," Toby said. "I give up: How is he going to be wrong?"

"When the diversion comes, we'll already be on board the Pool ship, working on breaking those access codes," I said. "The diversion won't be to cover us getting on. It'll be to cover the fact that we're already there."

It sounded good. Sounded like I had a plan. I didn't.

CHAPTER 4

I pulled Tobias and Marco aside after the council of war.

"Tobias? Did you notice that pillar of smoke off to the south of where we were?"

Tobias glared at me. <What you did to Cassie was beyond wrong.>

I squirmed. "I don't have time for that, Tobias."

<Cassie is one of us,> he said.

"Did you see the smoke or not?!" I demanded.

<Yeah.>

"Then I need you to go find out exactly where it's coming from. Now. I mean, if you can spare the time from busting me."

Tobias didn't answer. He just spread his wings and flapped till he cleared the trees and then caught a tailwind out of sight.

Marco gave me a fish-eyed look, but he didn't say anything.

"Marco, we need to know who is currently in charge of military forces in this area."

Marco thought that over. "It's not going to be just one guy. You'll have an air force general, a marine, an army guy."

I nodded. "Yeah. But the Pentagon will have given someone the weight, you know? Someone is going to be in overall command. I mean, if they haven't done that at least . . . they can't be that sorry, can they? I want you to get me a name and a location. Grab Ax. Use him to creep Pentagon computers or whatever it takes. I need the person who can give orders and have them followed in this area."

"How about the Chee? They'd be able to help us out."

I shrugged. "Where are the Chee? That's the problem. Those Bug fighters smoked the King house. I don't think it would have damaged their underground complex, but with the house gone how do we make contact?"

"Guess that's two problems for me and Ax," Marco said.

"Yeah." I hung my head. "I didn't mean to do

that with Cassie. It was . . . stuff happens sometimes."

"Uh-huh. I better get going."

In twenty-four hours I had two of the three an-
swers I was looking for. Marco did not find the
Chee. He did find what he hoped and believed
was the man in charge of military forces arrayed
against the Yeerks.

"He's an army general. Three star. His name
is Sam Doubleday. He's fifty-four years old. His
headquarters is fifty miles from here, though. In
the hills, some kind of nuclear shelter in a hol-
lowed out mountain."

"Good. At least he's not dumb enough to be
right here where the Yeerks can't help but kill
him."

The second piece of information was more in-
triguing.

<They're building a new Yeerk pool,> Tobias
reported. <Not so much a cave like the old one.
More like they're digging a small lake and going
to let it be open. Taxxons are all over the place,
like maggots on a piece of roadkill.>

I could see that Marco was preparing some
witty remark on the fact that Tobias was unusu-
ally familiar with roadkill. I shot him a look and
he sighed, letting it go.

A second Yeerk pool being built at a frantic

pace. That made sense. Once it was finished the Yeerks would remove the Pool ship back to safety in orbit. Taxxons were natural tunnelers, faster and more effective than anything Caterpillar made. It was like having a few hundred giant sentient earthworms at work.

"Okay," I said. "Let's go see this general."

<Who goes?> Tobias asked pointedly.

"Animorphs," I said. But of course I knew what he was asking. "All of us. I'll have James's people come in to watch the camp here. The rest of us, the six of us, we go to see the general. Wait, ask James to come, too. He can use the experience."

<Well, you'll need to go ask Cassie yourself,> Tobias said primly.

"Marco: Let everyone know. *Everyone.*" I avoided looking at Tobias. Not often do I feel like a coward, but I felt like one right then.

CHAPTER 5

They called it ATF-1. Alien Task Force One.

Their headquarters was a concrete-and-steel pit carved into a mountain. It was a sort of minor-league version of the big nuclear war fighting facility in Colorado. It had the look of a place that has just been brought out of mothballs. There were cobwebs hiding in the upper corners of the rooms. Dust was still being wiped from the sort of clunky computers and monochrome monitors you'd see in a video about the early days of the space race.

Inside the mountain were hundreds of soldiers and airmen, but mostly armed, it seemed, with clipboards and Palm Pilots. They wore the exactly ironed uniforms of bureaucrat-soldiers.

Outside the gaping mouth of The Hole, it was a different picture. Men were in firing positions on the tumbled, rocky slopes. Coming in as birds of prey again, we spotted machine-gun nests, tank emplacements, an artillery park well-camouflaged in the trees down the valley. Helicopters flew constant patrols.

Razor wire was going up everywhere. Soldiers were laying minefields on both sides of the only road.

Security was very tight — it took us no time at all to penetrate it. The general's men were looking for giant bug-eyed monsters from outer space. Not dragonflies.

We zoomed around the underground headquarters, locating storage vaults, some fairly impressive underground barracks, food-and-water storage, electronics, so on.

I located the general by watching the flow of uniforms. Lieutenants talked to captains, captains to majors, majors to colonels. My dragonfly eyes were good enough for me to spot colonels' bars. In time, the various colonels led me to the general.

He was in a map-walled conference room. I'd have smiled if I had a mouth. It was like something right out of a war movie: maps and phones and guys chomping cigars.

I landed on the conference table, right in the

middle of a large map of the city. The map showed a circle surrounding the former Yeerk pool. I guessed it was derived from satellite photos of what was left of my home town.

I demorphed.

"What the . . ."

"General!" someone yelped.

"MP's! MP's, on the double."

"Draw your weapons!"

"Don't shoot!"

There was a flurry of running men and cocking weapons and lots of shouting. I'd had quite an impact. Not a surprise. I was changing from a two-inch-long insect to a nearly six-foot-tall teenager.

My compound eyes grew huge, larger by far than my dragonfly body, before they bubbled up like overcooked marshmallows, melted, shrank, and finally re-formed into my own human eyes.

Of course they were human eyes staring out of a dragonfly's face.

The morphing process has never been the kind of neat, smooth, fluid thing you see in a computer-animated special effect. It's messier and weirder. Things grow or shrink at different speeds. Parts of one form linger long after the others have morphed. Ax could explain it, if you had an hour to listen.

What the general saw was a creature with human eyes and a twitching insect proboscis and gossamer wings and a largely human body.

I was probably lucky he didn't just order me to be shot. There were a dozen rifles and pistols aimed at me by the time I completed my de-morph.

"General Doubleday," I said. "My name is Jake."

"Get him!"

Three big, burly MP's were on me before I could yell. They knocked me onto my back, twisted me over on my face, and slapped hand-cuffs on me.

"General, this is a mistake," I yelled.

"Mistake, is it? Sure as death you're one of them," he said.

"No, sir, I'm not," I grated with my cheek pressed hard onto a pencil and a crumpled map. "But chances are some of the people in this room are."

"Let me shoot him," a major cried. Either a Controller or an idiot.

"Shoot him? Have you lost your senses, Ma-jor? This is a potentially valuable prisoner. Get my G-2 down here! Take him away, lock him up."

I sighed. The MP's hustled me from the room, down a hallway to a bare, overlit room furnished with a chair and a sink and a cot and a steel door with a feeding slot in it.

They threw me in, not at all gently.

I was a prisoner.

Three minutes later, I demorphed in front of General Doubleday again.

He had me tackled once more, handcuffed, shackled, my mouth duct-taped. I was carried, hog-tied, from the room and thrown back in the cell. In the cell I was chained to the cot.

Three minutes later, I demorphed in front of General Doubleday.

"General, why don't you stop being stupid and listen?" I said.

He stopped being stupid. But not until the fourth time I demorphed in front of him. And then, at last, he narrowed his eyes and looked at me and said, "All right, Mr. Alien, what have you got to say to me?"

"First: I'm not an alien. I'm a human with access to alien morphing technology. Second: I know how to hurt the Yeerks in a way that they won't be able to brush off, but I'll need your help to provide a diversion."

The general looked amused. "My help, huh? You need my help? See the stars on my shoulder there, son? I'm a major general, U.S. Army. You're a kid who can turn into a bug. I take my orders from the chain of command, and that ain't you."

It was a nice try, but I've been intimidated by

the best. After you stand up to the likes of Andalites, Visser One, and Crayak, you don't quiver just because some guy has stars on his shoulders.

"The chain of command is almost certainly infiltrated by Yeerks," I said. "So is this base. Probably even this room. You don't know if the orders you get are legitimate or not. You don't know if the orders you give out are going to be obeyed. Your power extends only as far as the first Controller in your staff."

The general's face was growing redder the more I talked. But, like I say, you want scary? Visser One has a tendency to morph into huge, murdering alien beasts. Red face? Not even in the game.

"Get out of my headquarters," Doubleday said.

"He can't leave here alive," said a middle-aged colonel who looked strangely like a Baldwin brother.

The Baldwin colonel nodded to one of the MP's. The MP drew his sidearm and chambered a round.

"Holster that weapon, soldier," the general snapped.

The MP leveled the gun at me.

"I said holster that weapon!" the general roared.

The MP ignored him and looked instead to the colonel. Two other officers drew weapons. One drew a bead on the general. The other stood ready, covering the rest of the room.

"I'd rather take him alive — the visser would be sure to reward us," the colonel mused. "On the other hand, if we let him escape, we're dead." He gave me a hard look. "Better safe than dead of Kandrona starvation. Shoot him."

"Now," I said.

From beneath the conference table a great, shaggy, gray-coated wolf exploded out and upward. Cassie's jaw closed around the MP's throat and carried him down to the ground.

A wolf's jaws are made for breaking the marrow out of bones. Those long, yellowed teeth digging into your throat, ready with a twitch to sever at least two major arteries, definitely get your attention.

Then the entire table went flying. It was a big, thick, mahogany thing, must have weighed five hundred pounds. But a gorilla is a strong animal.

Marco gave one of the Controllers a gorilla love tap that slammed him against the wall.

But perhaps most surprising to everyone were two low-ranking soldiers who calmly drew concealed weapons and pointed them at the Controllers. Continuing to hold the weapons Rachel and Ax demorphed.

31

The three Controllers were handcuffed and led away.

"You see my point, General," I said.

He nodded. He smoothed his ruffled hair. He pulled a cigar out of his pocket. "All right, son. Let's talk."

BOOM!

The concussion shook the room and threw me into the wall. There was blood pouring from my nose and ears and mouth.

BOOM!

Marco grabbed me before I could fall over again.

"Thanks, man."

<It's just never easy, is it?> he said.

CHAPTER 6

BOOM! BOOM!

Explosion followed explosion in rapid sequence. Every time I tried to get organized the concussion would knock me silly again.

"Marco! Take care of the general!" I managed to yell.

I started to morph. Tiger. "We're gonna be up to our butts in Hork-Bajir!" I warned everyone. They knew what to do.

I heard gunfire. Lots of it.

Should have seen this coming. Should have known the Yeerks would be wired into this headquarters. Someone, some Controller, had put in the call to Visser One: They're here. The Animorphs are here.

No, wait. Maybe not. Maybe they were just assaulting the base without knowing we were here. In which case it was just a typically crude Visser-One move.

Ax had demorphed. In his Andalite form he was a blue-furred centaur with a pair of extra eyes on movable stalks and a tail like a chef's knife tied to the end of a bullwhip. Rachel and Tobias were both well into morphing Hork-Bajir. When fighting Hork-Bajir-Controllers there is nothing quite as useful as having a few of our own to confuse things.

"Let me up," General Doubleday raged at Marco. "I have to go to my men."

<Let him up, Marco. General: Do you have any kind of surveillance cameras set up in this place?>

"What? Is that you? Are you some kind of a tiger now?"

<Yeah, some kind. General, if you have security cameras, turn them on. We can use the tape later to spot the safe guys. Anyone who shoots a Controller is someone we can trust.>

The general nodded. "The cameras are always on. Now get out of my way."

He motioned a sergeant to open the door leading out into the main chamber of the underground redoubt. The sergeant took up a firing position half in and half out of the doorway. A Dracon beam annihilated the half of him that was exposed.

The general caught his gun as it dropped. "We have to get out of here. This room is a trap."

I agreed. <Rachel. Go.>

Rachel leaned her bladed, goblin head gingerly out of the doorway and yelled, <Stop shooting, you fools.>

The firing continued, but it was no longer directed at our doorway. Rachel and Tobias stalked angrily out and berated the lead elements of the Hork-Bajir assault force.

"We have the *gafrash* human general, you *loglafach*. The visser wants him alive, and if you kill him it'll be you the visser eats for breakfast!"

Even less firing now.

Then a suspicious human voice, a human-Controller, demanding, "Which unit are you two with?"

<Ax then me then Marco and Cassie with the general,> I said tersely.

Ax leaped through the doorway. I was a millisecond behind him. There were forty or so Hork-Bajir and half a dozen obvious human-Controllers waiting for us. Some kept up fire down one hallway and upward at a catwalk lined with soldiers.

There was a full second of stunned immobility as they absorbed the sudden appearance of an Andalite.

"Andalite!" someone yelled.

<Surprise,> Ax said. He's almost developed a sense of humor. Almost.

But by then Ax was in the midst of them, slashing with his deadly tail. I came in after him. The bigger the crowd, the better: hard to use Dracon beams when your own people are all around.

Hork-Bajir slashed at me. I felt cuts on my flanks, my back. My tail was suddenly gone. My tiger's brain registered every wound but dismissed them, set aside the pain. This was a dominance fight. Tiger instinct and human will combined in me to press the attack forward.

I roared back, launched into my nearest tormentor, and smacked his horned head with a blow that could stun an elephant. I spun and gutslashed another. I closed my teeth on a flailing arm and worried it savagely like a mad dog with his last bone.

I was in the tiger and the tiger was in me. No time to think, only act and react. Cat speed. Cat accuracy. But the sheer weight of the attackers would defeat Ax and me, and even in the battle frenzy, I knew it.

Rachel and Tobias had joined the fight, but now, Hork-Bajir themselves, their abilities were no greater than those of their opponents.

<The general's clear!> Marco yelled in thought-speak. <We're coming.>

<No! Stay with him!> I ordered.

BamBamBam!

The volume of firing increased suddenly. I caught a wild, distorted vision of troops lined up on the catwalk pouring automatic fire down on us.

I heard Doubleday's foghorn voice bellowing, "Don't hit the tiger or the blue thing!"

<Rachel! Tobias! Back off, get outta here and morph something else. You'll get shot.>

A Hork-Bajir nailed me with a sudden, unexpected blow. No pain, just a shocking numbness. My hind legs collapsed. He had severed my spine. The bottom half of the tiger's body might as well be gone.

I would be dead in seconds. Had to demorph. No other choice.

BamBamBamBamBamBam!

Demorph, Jake, I told myself, already loopy, drifting. *Demorph.*

A huge Hork-Bajir stood tall above me. The tiger's blood dripped from his wrist blade. He raised his T. Rex foot. He was going to gut me, make sure I was dead. Couldn't move my body. My front paws batted feebly at the air. Helpless.

Half a dozen rounds caught him in the chest. He fell straight back.

I lay there, twisted halfway around, a tiger

pretzel. Ax was now astride me, whipping like a mad thing, a Cuisinart making Hork-Bajir puree.

I heard a thud. Bullet in my hindquarters. I looked up, confused, unable to focus clearly. Then my vision cleared enough to see a soldier drawing careful, deliberate aim at me. A Controller. He looked just like his fellow soldiers, but he wasn't shooting at the Hork-Bajir, he was going for a head shot on me, that's what he was going for.

He fired. I saw the muzzle flash.

I felt the bullet hit the right side of my head. But I wasn't dead.

Something big and brown came barreling through, sweeping Hork-Bajir before it. Ax was no longer above me, but was shoulder-to-shoulder with a grizzly bear. Cassie ran, bounded up, bounced off Rachel's massive shoulders and took a wild, flying leap straight into the Hork-Bajir.

The Hork-Bajir were falling back.

And still, I could see that single soldier biting his lip and taking aim at me again. This time he wouldn't miss. I was isolated, alone, defenseless. No one saw. No one could possibly see that he was aiming at me, not at the Hork-Bajir.

I could see his finger tighten on the trigger.

He was too focused to notice the gray-and-white blur as the falcon raked his face, leaving great gashes across his nose and forehead.

I was wrong: A falcon could see a man's eyes and know where they were aimed.

<Thanks, James,> I said, loopy and fading fast. <That was very nice of you.>

Marco was over me, shaking me with big gorilla hands and yelling, <Demorph! Demorph!>

Demorph?

Oh . . . okay.

CHAPTER 7

Doubleday listened after that. He evacuated his headquarters at top speed. The Yeerks would be back, especially now that they knew we were there. Fortunately, like a good general, he had a fallback position.

I explained about the three days, how no Yeerk can survive for more than three days without consuming Kandrona rays in a Yeerk pool.

"You need to lock down yourself and your officers and as many men as you can for three days. Whoever is left after that will be reliable."

"I've got two regular army divisions and half a dozen guard units under my command. I can't lock down and watch anything like that number of men."

"General, better a hundred men you can trust than ten thousand you can't."

He agreed. Unfortunately, this meant a three-day delay before he could provide the diversion we needed to take the Pool ship. In that time the Yeerks, with all their Taxxons, might well get the new Yeerk pool up and running. It wouldn't be finished, most likely, but if it was at all functional, if it could be used to feed the Earth-based Yeerks, I was certain that Visser One would fly his precious Pool ship back up into the safety of orbit.

So we had to make sure the new Yeerk pool wasn't ready. Which meant two impossible missions instead of just one.

Better and better.

"At least it'll be mostly Taxxons," Marco said when we were all back at camp and eating a meal of dry cold cereal. "They're easy to take down. Once they're injured at all, they're dead: Their brother Taxxons make sure of that."

Taxxons are like big, nasty caterpillars or centipedes. As big around as an old oak tree. They walk on rows of needle legs, carrying the upper third of their bulk erect. They have a ring of red-jelly eyes and a lamprey mouth. And they are hungry as shrews: always hungry. Always. It's a madness, a raging, insatiable need.

The Yeerks had bought them off and made them allies by the simple expedient of promising to feed them. Some Taxxons carried the Yeerk slug in their feverish brains, but many did not. The Yeerks hated them as host bodies, hated living with the hunger that not even a Yeerk could control.

And then, there was the danger that Marco had alluded to: Taxxons are cannibals. A wounded Taxxon is almost always set upon by his brothers, even in the middle of battle. It's like watching sharks react to blood in the water.

"Yeah, they're easy to kill," I said, feeling the dark, bitter gloom that always came over me after a battle. "But they'll be protected by Hork-Bajir and by Bug fighters. And by human-Controllers, of course."

"We blew up one Yeerk pool," Rachel said cockily. "So we blow up another. Badda-boom. Nothing to it."

She knew better, of course. She was just playing her part. Not for the first time I wondered what on Earth would happen to her if this war ever ended. Off to college to study prelaw or whatever? She was the goddess of war, my cousin was. Sixteen years old and a veteran of more battles than a World War II veteran. So was I, but Rachel loved it in a way I didn't. She needed it.

"Anyone have any useful suggestions?" I asked. It was just us, just the Animorphs. I'd had it with councils of war. "Tobias? You've seen the place."

<It's a big hole in the ground. Looks like a strip mine or something. It's sort of terraced: a series of shelves stepping down to what will be the pool itself. The "shore," I guess you'd call it, is maybe a hundred feet wide. The pool is going to be three hundred feet across, give or take. Not deep: maybe eight feet, almost flat on the bottom, but graded so it can be drained for repair. The terraces higher up, two of them, as I recall, are more like twenty feet wide.>

<Those will eventually be weapons emplacements,> Ax suggested. <It was the central flaw of the old pool: They never had a serious set of internal defenses. They will ring the pool with Dracon cannons able to reach up, across, or down.>

"Just for us," Rachel said with a laugh. "It's kind of flattering."

"How do you hurt a hole in the ground?" Marco wondered.

<Cave in the sides?> Tobias suggested dubiously.

"With what?" Marco said.

Cassie started to say something, stopped herself. Then, gathering her courage, she blurted, "You can't worry about the hole, you have to destroy the digging equipment."

43

I raised an eyebrow. "The equipment is Taxxons."

She looked away.

Marco whistled softly. "Yep," he agreed, nodding respectfully at Cassie.

Was Cassie just stating the obvious, or was she trying to reestablish herself by being as ruthless as any of us?

Either way, she was right: Forget the dirt, focus on the shovels. There was not an endless supply of Taxxons. I wished I knew how many there were, altogether. Once again I mourned the loss of access to the Chee, our most valuable sources of information.

"Okay," I said. "So we go after the Taxxons. I better go see Toby. Cassie? Go see James and his people. We'll need everyone we can get. We go tonight."

"Oh, man, I'm just getting over this morning's fun," Marco complained.

"Eat your dry, stale granola," Rachel said with a laugh. "You need to keep up your strength."

CHAPTER 8

At the beginning of the American Civil War both sides thought the war was about taking or holding cities and ports and rivers and mountain passes. They thought it was a chess game.

By the end of the war they'd figured out that they weren't playing chess. Cities didn't matter much. Ports and rivers and mountain passes, while useful, were secondary to the real game. The real game was destruction.

Lincoln had figured it out earlier than most and his generals; Ulysses S. Grant, William Tecumseh Sherman, and Philip Sheridan made it happen.

They burned enemy homes and farms. They burned crops in the field and slaughtered farm animals and wrapped railroad tracks around trees. They starved the enemy.

They realized that warfare was no longer about chivalry and honor, but about killing the enemy. Find the enemy, kill the enemy. Kill so many of them that those who are left alive lose their will to fight on. Do whatever it takes.

That's the way war has been ever since.

For a long time we had fought the Yeerks reactively. We were always ten steps behind, trying to foil this plan or that plan. We'd tried to fight the war with at least some vestige of decency. And maybe that had been okay when we were fighting to stop an infiltration. Now things were different. We were down to the final stages. Either the Yeerks would prevail, or we would.

So I gave simple orders to my people, the original Animorphs, and the auxiliary Animorphs, and Toby's free Hork-Bajir. Orders I had never given before: Kill the enemy. Kill the Taxxons.

Dress it up however you want, that's what war is about. If there's glory in there somewhere, I must have missed it.

We Animorphs went in first, the six of us, in bat morph. Tobias had reported that real bats were in the area during the evening hours, which would allow us to blend in naturally.

Flying as a bat is very different from flying as

a bird. You never feel that the air is your natural home. You always feel that you're airborne only by virtue of hard work, and if you let up for an instant you'll drop like a rock. It's not actually quite that bad, but that's how it feels.

Bats can see just fine, contrary to what some people think. They're not owls or hawks, but they see. But it's the echolocation that sets them apart.

It's like a sort of Etch-A-Sketch picture of the world. You fire off a series of ultrasonic clicks. The sound waves bounce off objects, are picked up by your ears, and are translated in your bat brain into a sort of alternate reality picture of the world around you.

You "see" things you don't see with your eyes. You see insects in flight as tiny pinpoint meteorites. And you overlook other things. But working together, regular sight and echolocation, once you relax into it and let the bat's brain work it out, you get a very complete picture.

We had approached within a quarter mile of the site before morphing. Then we split up and moved in from different angles, flying wild and jerky, flapping our skin wings, blasting our unheard radar sounds all around.

The Bug fighters swooped overhead, oblivious to us. Huge spotlights shone down from the lip of

the hole. Heavily armed men and Hork-Bajir pa-
trolled. They were very much on guard. No one
was napping.

And down inside, just like Tobias had said,
like worms after a heavy rain, the Taxxons worked.

There were pieces of heavy equipment down
there as well: earthmovers, cranes, graders, and
so on. But the Taxxons were digging up the dirt,
squirming their way into walls of gravel and dirt
and rock with amazing speed.

As we watched a large section of slope collapsed inward. The Taxxons had tunneled beneath it, loosened the structure and allowed it to
fall in on them. They seemed to suffer no permanent damage as they wormed free. Taxxons are
easy to cut, not easy to squash, perfectly adapted
to their own ecological niche.

<There are more Taxxons than meet the eye,> I
warned everyone. <No way to know how many are
belowground in tunnels. Be on guard for that: They
may come swarming up from underneath us.>

<I'm more worried about those Bug fighters,>
Marco said. <What if they decide the Taxxons are
expendable? What if they decide to start shooting?>

<Unlikely, but they may if they figure the
Taxxons are toast anyway,> I agreed. <If they do,
take cover in the Taxxon holes. Any other questions?>

No one said anything. I was braced for something from Cassie. Surely she would raise some sort of moral objection to this straightforward slaughter. But she remained silent. Hard to know what she would object to. It was always a question of balance for her, I guess. She was committed to winning, believed in our cause, understood that there would be terrible things to be done. But she found some things, and not other things, to be over the line. Me, I barely knew where the line was anymore. I'd come to depend on Cassie to keep me from going too far.

Nothing from Cassie.

<Okay. See that vertical rift over on the right there? Looks deep and dark enough for us. We go in. Then, battle morphs, and come out hot and mean. Soon as we're engaged I'll signal James. Then, Toby.>

We swooped silently down, down through the hazy lights and into the deep cleft that, to our bat senses, was well defined and perfectly clear.

<Ax first,> I ordered. Ax had only to demorph to be dangerous. The rest of us had to demorph, then morph again.

With Ax ready I began to demorph. As my weight returned I had to grab exposed roots with unformed hands to keep from sliding down the cleft. Then, morphing to tiger, I lost my hold and slid, tumbling down.

I rolled to a stop by Ax who waited calmly just within the shadow. A pair of Taxxons toiled not ten feet away, out in the hazy light. They hadn't seen or smelled us.

My acute tiger senses told me even without looking that the others were morphed behind me.

<Three count,> I said more calmly than I felt. <Three, two, GO!>

It must have been a terrifying sight for the Taxxons. An Andalite warrior and five wild beasts suddenly roaring out of a crack in the dirt wall. The nearest Taxxons had no chance to react. We hit them, slashed, cut, and moved on, knowing that a wounded Taxxon is a dead Taxxon.

I moved at breakneck speed. Slashed the nearest Taxxon, leaped atop him, propelled myself away, digging my hind claws into him for good measure.

I hit the ground, took two loping steps, and was ripping the next Taxxon before he could scream.

But now the Taxxon voices were crying out in their shrill, sibilant language.

"Sreeeeya! Ansacaleees!"

I caught a glimpse of a wild African elephant burying ivory tusks in a Taxxon's raised chest. Rachel tossed her head and the tusks nearly removed the top third of her victim.

Marco in cheetah morph and Ax fought most

logically. They each understood that a mere wound was enough, as long as live Taxxons were left undamaged to take care of the finishing off. Marco would accelerate to forty mph, dig his less-than-deadly claws into a victim, leave bloody scratches behind, and prance away far too quickly for a Taxxon to respond.

Ax wielded his tail with the precision of a surgeon. Tobias wheeled and dove at the red jelly eyes. And Cassie was there, too, in wolf morph, tearing into sausage-casing flesh, ripping and jumping back.

It was a sheer, one-sided massacre.

Now the security forces, human-Controller and Hork-Bajir, were getting into the game. They came running around the lip of the crater to get close enough to fire down into us without hitting the Taxxons.

<Here they come,> I warned.

But we were faster than the Taxxons, and, with the exception of Rachel, smaller. Excited Hork-Bajir firing wildly were doing almost as much damage as we were.

"Don't stand up here shooting, get down there!" a human voice bawled. "Get down there, you cowards!"

<James!> I yelled. <Now!>

Clear across the crater, James and seven of his people in morph erupted amid the Taxxons.

That would keep the security forces from concentrating.

Taxxons were running away, turning and running, confused, terrified. Others lacked even that much self-control: They fell upon their wounded brothers and slammed their teeth-lined round mouths down again and again, reared up high, and with a *"Sreee!"* of delight tore chunks from their still-living fellow Taxxons.

I saw two wounded Taxxons devouring each other. Both screamed in rage and hate; both must have known, somewhere, deep in their fevered minds, that this was madness, but neither could stop.

<Ax! Hork-Bajir behind you!> I yelled.

Unnecessary, of course: An Andalite sees in all directions at once.

But now the easy part was definitely over: Hork-Bajir were piling into the melee. It was the difference between fighting big, nasty but vulnerable worms and fighting walking razor blades.

A Hork-Bajir leaped over a fallen Taxxon and landed right in front of me. Just that morning I'd let a Hork-Bajir cut me down.

<Not this time,> I said, and launched myself straight at him, straight for his face. At arm's length a Hork-Bajir is almost the equal of a tiger. At close range the tiger is king.

I broke free and yelled, <Okay, Toby, your turn! Now!>

The battle had drawn every Yeerk eye down to the pit. The swift, running approach of sixty free Hork-Bajir warriors had gone unnoticed, even by the buzzing, frustrated Bug fighters overhead.

The Yeerks were uncoordinated, thrown off by our successive waves. Our plan was working. But sooner or later someone was going to take charge of the shocked and off-balance Yeerks.

Two minutes more, I told myself, *and we bail.*

It was one minute too many. The Bug fighters opened fire without warning. They fired on Taxxon and human-Controller and Hork-Bajir alike.

More Bug fighters were maneuvering to get into firing position. They were going to kill everyone, friend and foe alike. They were doing our work for us. But we would surely die as well.

Hork-Bajir-Controllers were running for it, scrambling up out of the pit.

<Toby! Mix your people in with them and run! James! Fall back. We'll distract them for another few seconds.>

<We get all the fun jobs,> Marco muttered.

And then, what I had warned against, had foreseen . . . and forgotten. The ground opened beneath me and I fell.

CHAPTER 9

<Aaahhh!>

I fell a long way. My tiger speed and balance turned me around, aimed my feet down, tail twirling to maintain this attitude.

I hit the dirt, took the shock in all four paws, rolled sideways, and came up snarling. Snarling at nothing. I was in an empty tunnel. Dark. Too dark for even my cat's eyes. But I smelled plenty, a smell I knew: Taxxon.

I stayed on guard, not too worried, but definitely ready. I heard a sound . . . shuffling, grinding . . . digging!

The ground opened beneath me again and I fell in a cascade of dirt, down, and this time no hard landing on a flat surface. I was in a chute, rolling, trying to grab on with my spike claws. But the surface was smooth, almost like glass. And now I was getting worried.

I fell for only thirty seconds or so, but that's a long way to go underground. Finally the chute ended and I was once more rolled across a dirt floor.

<Marco! Rachel!> No answer. Was I that far underground? Out of thought-speak range? I took a chance. <Marco, get everyone home, that's an order. Don't argue.>

There was light. Dim, but more than enough for me.

And there were Taxxons: three of them. Each carried a Dracon beam in one set of upper legs. I could get one, maybe two of them. But three? Before they could shoot me?

<Please do not attack, we mean you no harm.>

It was thought-speak! Not the impossible-to-decipher hissing and spitting of spoken Taxxon. Thought-speak, and impossible as it seemed, I had the strangest impression that it was an Andalite thought-speak "voice."

I froze.

<What do you want?> I demanded.

<To speak to you, Jake.>

He knew my name. Of course the Yeerks did know my name now, but still it was a shock.

<Okay, so speak. You've got the Dracon beams, I guess I'll listen.>

The Taxxon who was speaking opened his pincers and let the Dracon weapon drop. The other two did the same.

<Now we are at your mercy, Animorph. That morph is more than capable of killing the three of us.>

I took a deep breath. <Okay, let's talk. You know me. Who are you?>

<My name is Arbron. I am — was — an Andalite *aristh*.>

<You're a Taxxon.>

<Your friend Tobias is a hawk,> he countered.

<You're stuck in morph? You're a morphed Andalite stuck as a Taxxon? A *nothlit?*> I couldn't keep the horror out of my voice. One thing to be trapped as a hawk. But to be trapped as a Taxxon?

<I am a Taxxon,> Arbron said almost proudly. <I have been for more years than I can easily count. I was on the Taxxon home world with two Andalites of your acquaintance. One was Alloran-Semitur-Corrass.>

<Visser One?>

<Not then. But, yes, Alloran became the unwilling host body for the Yeerk now ranked Visser One. He commanded our mission. Alloran was an Andalite prince with the smallest possible

command: two lowly *arisths.* Me, and Elfangor-Sirinial-Shamtul.>

I stopped breathing. Could it be possible? Elfangor, Ax's brother? Elfangor, who gave us the morphing power to begin with? This . . . this whatever he was had been a friend of Elfangor's?

<What do you want?> I asked him.

He shuffled closer and I had to resist the normal reaction of disgust.

<I want to be free, Jake the Animorph.>

<You're a Controller?>

<No. I have no Yeerk within me. We want to be free . . . we all want to be free . . . of the curse of being Taxxons.>

<I don't understand,> I said, although I was beginning to guess.

<The morphing power,> Arbron said, now sounding almost desperate. <The morphing power! Don't you see? If the Taxxons could morph, acquire some more benign shape and find a safe haven on your planet . . . become something other than what they are, escape the hunger. You cannot imagine the hunger . . . they've seen that there could be a better way. The virus of knowledge is in their bloodstreams now, they realize that they could change forever!>

<You're telling me the Taxxons want to . . . to stop being Taxxons?>

<Yes. Yes. My people have seen a better

57

way . . . a way out of this life of eternal, excruciating pain and hunger, a hunger that has made us slaves of the Yeerks.>

I didn't know what to say. Too much to absorb. An entire species wanting to morph? And surely Arbron knew that we no longer had the morphing cube, that Visser One had it. And in any event, Arbron must know that it wouldn't work on him. Not on a *nothlit.*

As if he was reading my mind, Arbron said, <Listen to me, Jake the Animorph. I have been a leader of these, my new people, for many years. We have fought the hunger, resisted as well as we could the murderous cannibalistic urges. I've tried to show them a better way. But the need is too powerful. Resistance always breaks down, and we fall again under Yeerk sway. They feed us, you see. It's as simple as that.

<I know that . . . I understand the morphing technology. I know it cannot save me, that I am forever trapped. But it can save my people. And if they are saved I can lay down my burden of leadership.>

No choice but to be honest, I thought. *I can't sustain a lie. I can't trick them.* <I don't have the morphing cube,> I said.

<We know. Visser One has it, and he will never free us, never. No Taxxon or even Taxxon-Controller has been allowed to acquire the mor-

phing power. We can only have it, only be free, if you and not the Yeerks are victorious.>

<And you would . . .> I began, not daring even to complete the sentence, it was too amazing, the possibilities too incredible.

<Yes. We would fight with you. There are one thousand seven hundred and nine non-Controller Taxxons on the surface of this planet and aboard the Pool ship. And we Taxxons would fight with you.>

CHAPTER 10

They had given me up for dead back at the valley of the free Hork-Bajir, so when I came flying in at first light there was a certain amount of amazement.

Not that Marco was going to make a big thing of it. "Oh, there you are," he said. "So I guess I can't have your CD collection after all."

I landed on the ground and demorphed as Cassie came running up, her tear-streaked face bright. She stopped herself from hugging me, and then turned away.

"Cassie. Stay. Please," I said. "Marco: Did we lose anyone last night?"

"Yeah. Three of Toby's people. One of James's

people, the guy named Ray. And you, or so we thought."

I had demorphed fully. I sat down hard. Ray was a kid born with severe birth defects. He'd acquired a leopard as his main morph. He loved the physical grace of the animal, a grace he'd never experienced in his human body.

"How are they taking it, James's people?"

"About like we were taking your death, Jake: not well. At least it was quick: Dracon beam. He never knew what hit him."

"We took out a lot of Taxxons," Rachel said, arriving on the scene impeccably dressed, looking like she'd just stepped out of an exclusive day spa despite the fact that it was not yet six in the morning and she, like all of them, had spent the night in one of the hasty, shabby log shacks we'd built.

"Was it worth it?" Cassie wondered, then looked as if she wished she'd kept her mouth shut.

I got up and went to her. I took her hands and said, "This time, yes. I think it was. Rachel? Round everyone up: Toby, the parents, the whole war council."

"Yeah?" she asked with an inquisitive look.

"They've got fifteen minutes to dress, pee, and drink a cup of roots n' twigs coffee." I laughed. I was feeling incredible. Feeling, despite the lack of sleep, despite the aftermath of two terrible battles in one day, wild and alive.

It took them twenty minutes, but that was okay. Okay aside from the fact that Marco tortured me for the secret the whole time.

At last the frowsy, discontented bunch was assembled.

"You're alive," Rachel's mom said, not seeming too happy about it.

"He's hard to kill," Marco said, shaking his head as though commiserating with her. "I've been tempted repeatedly during the last twenty minutes or so."

<I am very happy to see you alive, Prince Jake. But why have I been pulled away from finishing my morning rituals?> Ax said. He's cranky till he gets a few good hoofsfull of dewy grass.

I didn't know where to begin. I thought about dragging it out and making a production out of it, but this was a dangerously tired, discontented crowd and I was too full of the news to keep it bottled up.

"Well," I said, trying to sound laconic, "the Taxxons want to defect. They want to change sides."

Everyone just stared.

"Come again?" Cassie's dad said.

"The Taxxons. They want to join us. They're ready to turn against the Yeerks."

The parents for the most part didn't get it. Toby did. And Eva, the former Visser One.

My fellow Animorphs just stared in dumb, openmouthed, it-can't-be, no-way shock.

All but Cassie, who sighed as if she'd been holding her breath for weeks.

I went to her and said, "You knew, didn't you?"

She shook her head. "I hoped, that was all. I hoped."

"Pretty good hope, Cassie," I whispered.

"Oh my God," Marco said, getting it now. "It's the morphing. That's it, isn't it? The Yeerks got a taste of morphing. The Taxxons have figured out they could do it, too."

I nodded. "Yeah. The Taxxons grabbed me to talk to me. They're led by an Andalite *nothlit,* trapped in Taxxon morph. He said his name is Arbron. He said he was a former companion of Elfangor's."

Ax jerked visibly. <Arbron? It is a name from a very long time ago. But yes, an *aristh* named Arbron was a friend of my brother's.>

I recounted the details of the meeting, playing to a very, very attentive audience.

<You *believed* him?> Tobias asked.

I shrugged. "It doesn't make any sense as a trap. They had me dead. If they wanted to trap us, if it was all a setup, they'd have demanded I

63

return with all of you. They didn't. They told me to come back alone. Arbron wants me to speak to his people. He wants me to tell them what I told him. He wants my personal promise."

"Your promise of what?" Toby asked.

I looked right at Ax. "They want to be made morph-capable. They have contact with Yeerks who've morphed, and they are bitterly ticked that Visser One has refused to enable any of his Taxxon so-called allies. They realize we don't have the morphing cube anymore. And Arbron is smart enough to know that even if we win we may not get the cube from Visser One. He could escape with it or even destroy it. But they've realized that the Yeerks will never, ever allow them to gain morphing capabilities because it would be the end of Taxxon dependence on the Yeerks."

"So they want us to promise Andalite cooperation?" Marco said thoughtfully. "They want us to guarantee that the Andalites will pay off on our debt?"

I nodded. "Exactly. They want us to commit the Andalite high command to make every Taxxon morph-capable. In exchange, each Taxxon will choose a form and turn *nothlit.*"

<My people will never agree,> Ax said bluntly. <The morphing technology is the crown jewel of Andalite science. They are already furious that it has spread as far as the five of you and Visser

One. They do not know that Tobias's mother is morph-capable. They do not know about the auxiliary Animorphs. They do not know that the Yeerks have a cube. They will absolutely refuse.>

"Even if it means stopping a war, saving a planet, and disarming their greatest enemy?" Cassie asked. "Are they that stubborn? That stupid?"

Ax's main eyes flashed. <What they will say is that it is a trick: that the Yeerks are using the Taxxons to acquire more morphing power and become even more formidable foes.>

"They've said they'll go *nothlit* under our supervision," I said. "Permanent morph."

"The Andalite high command is not going to trust us that far," Marco said.

"The Andalite high command can drop dead," Rachel said. "What good have they ever been to us? Where are they, huh? We've always been their last priority. They've done squat for us. They're sitting off at a safe distance waiting to see whether we win or lose. If we win they'll pat us on the head and say, 'Good inferior species, good girl, here's a doggie treat.' And if we lose what are they going to do?"

No one had an answer to that. Then Cassie said, "Ax, you need to tell them."

Ax looked startled. His stalk eyes jerked toward Cassie.

"It's time to choose, Ax," Cassie said very quietly. "Once and for all. We all know what Alloran did to the Hork-Bajir world, trying to keep them from falling into Yeerk hands. The Andalites won't allow Earth to fall to the Yeerks, will they?"

CHAPTER 11

All attention was on Ax.

It was a long time before he spoke. It's hard to read Andalite emotions — they lack mouths, and that makes them less expressive than humans. But it was easy enough to guess at the conflicts going on inside that wonderfully quick, agile brain.

<I have at times contacted the Andalite fleet without telling anyone,> Ax said slowly.

"I'll kill you myself!" Rachel erupted.

"Rachel," I said as evenly as I could.

<There is a possibility that the Andalite high command might resort to . . . extreme measures.>

"Now can I kill him?" Rachel demanded.

I wasn't far from letting her. I was furious. Betrayed! Ax had used our limited communicator to chat with his people? Behind our backs?

Cassie said, "Ax has already defied them. They ordered him to stop our attack on the Yeerk pool. He disobeyed."

<You spied on me?> Ax asked her.

"I'm an Animorph, Ax," Cassie answered. "A flea on your back when you would sneak out of camp."

"Why on God's green Earth would these Andalites order him to stop us from killing their enemies?" Rachel's mother asked, and for once it was a good question.

Eva had the answer. "I can guess: They didn't want anything to stop the Yeerks from concentrating their forces here. They wanted the Yeerks to pour into Earth." She laughed mirthlessly. "The Yeerks are evil, destructive, dangerous creatures, I know that better than anyone. But the Andalites are no saints themselves. They want the Yeerks to concentrate here because the Andalites have written us off, decided we can't win, and they wanted to blast the entire planet out of existence and take out the bulk of the Yeerk race along with the human race."

"Is that true, Ax?"

Another long hesitation. Then, <Yes, Prince Jake. It is true.>

In a few moment's time I'd gone from the heights of hope and optimism to the depths of rage and despair. The Andalite fleet wasn't coming to rescue us. They were coming to destroy us in order to destroy the Yeerks.

In a heartbeat we'd lost one enemy, the Taxxons, and gained another, far more deadly: our erstwhile friends, our long-awaited saviors, the Andalites.

<How do we stop them, Ax-man?> Tobias asked. He and Ax are best friends.

"You're asking him?" Rachel raged, stabbing an accusing finger at the Andalite.

Ax held his head high and for a moment I thought he might refuse to answer Tobias's question. Then, <You must understand that the Andalite high command is not the entire Andalite electorate. This long war has made them a greater part of our civilization than they should rightly be. The Andalite electorate, the people, do not know what is planned.>

"So, how do we tell them?" Marco said. "Any time we dial up that communicator my dad invented it just reaches the Andalite fleet."

<We take the Yeerk Pool ship,> Ax said. <We use its power to contact the nonmilitary Andalite

communications net. We tell the Andalite people what has happened, what we've done, and what we have promised the Taxxons.>

<Will the Andalite people back us?> Tobias asked.

Ax looked grim. <Will your people? Will they allow Taxxons to morph and live in peace on this planet? Will your people choose trust over hatred and revenge?>

That put it back in my court. I didn't have an answer.

"Arbron wants me to speak to the Taxxons tonight," I said. "He's suggested I appear in morph — to demonstrate the possibilities. He doesn't know much about Earth animals. But he thinks the Taxxons would prefer something not too different from their current forms. Something strong but something not afflicted by the Taxxon hunger. Cassie?"

She looked blank. "Something similar to their present forms? Centipedes? Caterpillars? No, they'd want a longer lifespan at least. And you said strong . . . ah. I have an idea. I don't know. Maybe . . . I don't know. I'd be guessing."

I said, "Cassie, you guessed that letting Tom take the morphing cube might weaken rather than strengthen the Yeerks. You guessed that Ax was . . ." I stifled the most bitter word that came to mind. ". . . conflicted. I'll back your guess any day of the week."

"I think he means he's sorry he doubted you and treated you like crap," Rachel said archly.

"Yeah. That's exactly what I mean. Come on, Cassie, show me where to go next."

CHAPTER 12

"Is it a python?" I guessed.

"Anaconda," Cassie said.

The Gardens had survived the destruction of the town since it was outside the radius of annihilation. But it was closed. A handful of dedicated people worked to keep the animals from starving, but the place was a mess: The breeze blew trash around the usually pristine sidewalks; the whole place reeked of uncleaned cages and habitats; water pressure had been cut off so the picturesque moats and ponds were scummed over.

The snake house looked about like it always did, though some of the display areas were dark. I guess snakes are low maintenance.

The snake I was staring at looked about a foot

thick and so long I couldn't begin to guess at its total size. It had a clearly delineated head and a sort of rough-edged diamond pattern to its scales.

It was either asleep or dead. Or very relaxed.

"The anaconda is part of the python family," Cassie said. "One of if not the biggest snake species on Earth. It hunts live prey, but snakes are far from the kind of hunger a Taxxon knows. They have very slow metabolisms. They can go a long time between meals."

I peered at the informational plaque. "Native to the Amazon jungle?" I laughed. "You're thinking ahead."

Cassie looked embarrassed, like I'd caught her doing something dishonest. "If we agree to give the Taxxons a place to live in freedom here on Earth, why not the rain forest? The agreement would stop destruction of the rain forest dead in its tracks."

I nodded. "Yes, it would. But is this . . ." I jerked my head toward the snake. "Is this the morph that would appeal to a Taxxon?"

Cassie shrugged. "I guess I don't figure Taxxons are big on imagination. I think they'd want something fairly close, as you said, to what they are now. But not some helpless worm or bug: They're used to a certain relative size."

"Uh-huh. You sure that snake isn't dead? I haven't seen it move yet."

"Well, you see what I mean: It would be different from the relentless demands of life for a Taxxon. There's a lot of sitting in the sun involved."

"Florida retirement for Taxxons."

"Yeah."

"Well, let's get this over with," I said reluctantly.

"It's perfectly safe," Cassie said condescendingly.

"It's a snake. It's a snake the size of palm tree."

"Come on." She put her arm through mine and drew me away toward the access corridor behind the cages.

We both went in and I knelt and touched the dry scales. Not slimy at all, but still creepy. I acquired the snake. Its DNA joined the DNA of how many species floating around in my blood? I couldn't even remember them all.

"When you do this morph your biggest problem will be staying awake," Cassie said.

I stood up, and for a moment tried to figure out how to say what I wanted to say.

"Cassie, you ever wonder what happens if we win? You ever think about that?"

"All the time."

"Nothing will ever be the same. People will

know the galaxy is full of life, full of intelligent species. We'll have this huge rush of technological change. There'll be nothing to stop us from being a space-traveling species. Humans on the moon, on Mars, maybe colonizing planets all around the galaxy. And there's the morphing technology. Can you imagine what that's going to mean?"

Cassie nodded. "I guess I don't think about that stuff so much. I guess I think more about us. You and me. And all of us."

I took her in my arms. The anaconda's habitat was probably not the most romantic place on Earth, but it felt safe. "You know I love you."

"I love you, too, Jake," she said, and put her head on my shoulder.

"I guess if we win, if we survive, maybe we should, you know, get married and all. I mean, eventually. I know we're young, but man, we've been through enough that it should count for a few extra years, shouldn't it?"

I don't know what I expected her answer to be, but I didn't expect her to start crying. And not tears of joy, either.

"I would like that . . . eventually," she said.

"But. But what?"

She sighed. "But, Jake, what are you going to be? What are you going to do?"

"Guess I thought I'd go to college," I said.

"And study what, Jake? Me, I'll go to college, I'll become a doctor. I'll never forget what's happened, I'll never even try, but I'll be able to slip back into a normal life. But you, Jake?"

I shrugged and released her and stood away a bit. "I'm not Rachel, you know. I didn't fall in love with the fight. I don't need it like she does. I do it, I try and do it well, but it's just a job, a duty." I tried to make a joke of it. "I mean, what do you think? The Pentagon is going to call me up and make me Chairman of the Joint Chiefs of Staff? I'm not even old enough to enlist as a private."

She didn't laugh. She just looked at me.

"Look, Cassie, when this is over I'll be done with it forever. I'll go back to school, get an education, go to basketball games, get a driver's license, go to college, figure out what it is I really want to do. And be with you. You and me."

She forced a smile. "A year after it ends, if it ends, if we win, a year afterward if you want to be with me, we'll talk about that again, okay?"

"I have to wait a year? Kind of harsh, isn't it?"

"Hey, if we get married, Marco isn't going to live with us, is he?" Cassie said, trying her best to jolly us both out of our dark moods.

It didn't work.

For the first time I could taste the faint possibility of actual victory, despite the probable Andalite betrayal. The Taxxons might be joining us! For so long I'd fought with no hope at all.

I should be excited.

I should be happy.

CHAPTER 13

Arbron had given me the place: a spot more than a mile away from the site of the new Yeerk pool. He had not told me positively, absolutely, to come alone. So, I brought backup, though not in any visible form.

I flew with fleas nestled deep in my feathers. Only Tobias remained in his true form, flying "cover."

I found the spot easily enough: a used car lot just outside the blast area. It was abandoned, of course. About half the cars had been stolen by looters, and of those that remained maybe a third were damaged in some way. But there, just as Arbron had told me, waited a yellow VW Beetle.

I landed and demorphed. It was a chilly night, especially for someone in nothing but morphing clothes. I was glad to climb into the VW. I sat behind the steering wheel and looked around, not knowing what to expect. The little bud vase was empty.

<What are we doing?> Marco asked from his location somewhere on my body.

"We're sitting here looking like a suspicious car thief," I answered. "Where are you guys, anyway? Where on my body did you end up after I demorphed?"

Rachel answered, <Gotta tell you, cousin, I don't know where we are exactly, and I don't really want to know.>

"Mmmm. Good point."

<Marco just bit you,> Ax reported. <If I understand the physiology of flea bites correctly, you will experience an itching sensation later, and then will know precisely where we were.>

"There's a pleasant thought," I said.

<Hey, there's a key in the ignition. See if the radio works,> Marco suggested.

I punched the power switch. It was set to a news channel. The announcer sounded tired. ". . . are saying at this hour that the looting has diminished in intensity. Numerous fires are still burning, but fire departments from as far as a hundred miles away are sending trucks and crews to —" I pushed preset buttons and tried for some music.

There was a rumbling. I turned off the radio. "Um . . . you guys feel that?"

<We're fleas, we feel everything,> Cassie said.

Tobias called down from high above. <I guess you guys know the ground is opening up, right?>

"Buckle your seat belts."

The ground vibrated beneath the car and I followed my own advice, drew the shoulder belt across, and clipped it just as the ground opened up and the car began to roll forward, down a sloping tunnel into the ground.

It was elegantly done: The tunnel had an almost flat floor, the walls close enough to make steering unnecessary. The car rolled free, scuffing the dirt walls from time to time. How far down, I couldn't be sure. Then I glanced in the rearview mirror: The tunnel was being collapsed behind me.

If it was a trap after all, it was a very good trap.

All at once I emerged into a huge open space. A cavern, tall and arched, and lit by dim artificial lights high overhead.

The car rolled to a halt. I closed my eyes to adjust to the gloom. I opened them again and had an impression of restless movement all around.

I closed my eyes and opened them once more and this time I saw the Taxxons, everywhere, all around the car, pressing close, red jelly eyes staring.

"We're here," I muttered.

<Good. I need to pee,> Marco said.

"I'm going to get out," I whispered.

I opened the door slowly. I stood up.

They were everywhere, a wall of Taxxons. More Taxxons than I could have imagined in my worst nightmare. Not dozens, hundreds.

Arbron — at least I hoped it was him — danced forward on his needle legs. He raised his upper third and loomed high above me.

I knew, or at least hoped, it was a friendly gathering. But these were Taxxons, after all. Taxxons, not even Taxxon-Controllers. In their natural state they were insane with hunger, and I was food.

<Please climb to the podium,> Arbron invited me and I noticed for the first time a sort of rock-and-dirt mound maybe ten feet high. I scrambled up, trying not to look scared, and moving very, very carefully so as not to scrape a knee or cut a finger.

Arbron rose part of the way behind me. Then he spread his upper rows of Taxxon arms wide and began addressing the crowd in the Taxxon speech.

I didn't understand a word of it, but the Taxxon multitude did. They hissed and slithered and made a trilling sound that could either be approval or rage.

From atop the mound, and with my eyes adjusted to the near-darkness, I could see them all. A sea of Taxxons. A huge underground cavern reeking of ammonia and seething with oversized, murderous centipedes.

Then Arbron began to speak to them in thought-speak, presumably for my benefit.

<Taxxons! Here is the human who leads the fight against the Yeerks. He and his warriors have killed many of our people.>

I must have gone several shades more pale at that. It seemed a strange way to introduce me.

<He and his warriors have defied the power of Visser One, the former Visser Three, for years. It was he and his warriors who destroyed the Yeerk pool and killed many Yeerks.>

The crowd liked that. They murmured in true Taxxon form, hissing and spitting and writhing. Impossible not to feel that I was sitting on some gigantic piece of rotting meat surrounded by huge maggots. Impossible to shake that image.

<He and his warriors are friends to the Andalites who possess the transforming power. This human> — he pointed at me with three of his arms — <can morph!>

Now the crowd grew quieter, more attentive, less excited, but very, very focused.

<I have brought this human here to speak to you, my people.>

I recognized my cue. I was about to start speaking, but it occurred to me that a visual aid would be helpful. So I spread my arms wide and reached deep inside myself for the DNA that would form the tiger.

I morphed slowly, slowly so they could all see. They watched the claws grow from my fingers, saw the orange-and-black fur rush across my body, muttered as I dropped forward onto all fours.

<You might want to warn us,> Rachel complained. <It's like an earthquake down here.>

Then, I began to demorph more quickly. And once I was human again I focused my thoughts on the dragonfly. I shrank, fell toward the ground like a man diving off a skyscraper. The dirt and rock rose to me, gravel becoming boulders. Gossamer wings sprouted from my back. Articulated insect legs erupted from my chest. Massive eyes swelled like balloons, popping out of my eye sockets, overwhelming my face. I could actually see the fleas clinging to my body.

<Everyone hang on, we're going airborne,> I notified my friendly fleas.

I fired my wings and zoomed just over the

heads of the Taxxons. Then back, to land atop my podium. I demorphed. And now, if Cassie was right, the *pièce de résistance.*

I formed a picture of the anaconda in my mind. The changes began. I saw my skin harden, dry out, crack into thousands of interlocked scales.

My eyes moved around my head but remained forward-focused. My face bulged out, stretched, out and out. My arms were shriveling at a shocking pace. I was a weird creature, half snake, half human, standing erect but armless. Then my legs went weak and I dropped flat on my belly before I could fall. My legs melted into the tail that was stretching out and out and out from my elongating spine.

I was ten feet long and still growing. Longer and longer, and without thinking I shortened the muscles on one side of my body and brought my length up to form a loose coil.

The anaconda's senses replaced my own. Vision faded, color dimmed, but awareness of motion intensified. It was like when you set your computer cursor to show trails: everything, anything that moved was infinitely more interesting than color or shape.

My tongue tasted the air and I received a download of data — temperature, humidity, the scent of Taxxon exhalations.

I let the Taxxons take a good, long look.

<This creature is called an anaconda,> I said. <It is the largest of snakes, powerful, dangerous when provoked. But as I feel its mind within my own, I know that it is calm, at peace, restful. It is unafraid. It longs for food, but it can resist, can control its hunger.>

The chamber was silent. The Taxxons stared, stared holes in me with their red jelly eyes.

<Very good,> Arbron said privately to me.

CHAPTER 14

Human once more, I addressed the Taxxon multitude.

"My name is Jake. I am the leader of the Animorphs. As Arbron told you, we have killed many Taxxons using the morphing power. But we are not the enemies of the Taxxons. We are the enemies of the Yeerks. And we have killed many Yeerks."

They liked that okay.

"The Andalites are our friends."

<Yeah, right,> Rachel said in private thought-speak.

"The Andalites are coming, and there may be a great battle. The Andalites may win. The Yeerks may win. If we and the Andalites win, you will be given the choice — to remain as you are, or to change, to find a new form, and live in peace and contentment here, in a special place. A homeland for the Taxxons . . . for Taxxons who are no longer haunted by the desperate hunger, no longer prey to the Yeerks."

I was lying. At least in part. Arbron was an Andalite, or had been: He had to know that the Andalites would resist ever turning the morphing power over to the hated Taxxons.

I cringed a little as I spoke, waiting for him to interrupt, to call me a liar. But he let me go on. And I painted the picture for the Taxxons: life without hunger, a life of safety and security, where they would live in peace among themselves, no more cannibalism.

And Arbron let me go on speaking.

"The question is: Can we and our Andalite friends defeat the Yeerks and bring on this new day?"

They waited for the answer. I gave it to them, feeling weirdly like a presidential candidate delivering a stump speech.

"We can defeat the Yeerks . . . if you join us. Animorph, Andalite, and Taxxon together, we can win."

The Taxxons didn't cheer, exactly, but they did send up a creepy whistling sound that reverberated around the chamber.

Arbron slithered up beside me and, to my surprise, dismissed them, told them all to get back to their work. Hundreds of Taxxons obediently turned away and began filing out of side tunnels like a football stadium crowd after the game.

I probably looked puzzled as I turned to Arbron. "Well?"

<Well, they have agreed. For now. They will follow my direction. For now.>

"Okay, then I guess we should get down to specifics," I said. "You know the Pool ship is here on Earth, on the surface. It's there to feed the Yeerks until they can finish —"

<Why don't you ask your friends to demorph? I'm sure they would be more comfortable.>

That stopped me. But there was no point in trying to lie. "Yeah, I guess they would."

Fleas leaped away from me, unseen by either of us, and moments later my friends began to appear, growing out of swollen, vile, armor-plated flea bodies.

<And now, my friend,> Arbron said.

I heard footsteps and peered into the darkness of an access tunnel.

"Well, good evening, everyone. It's an awfully pretty night to spend it all in a filthy Taxxon tunnel."

I knew the voice. I'd heard it every day of my life. My brother. Tom.

My brother, the human-Controller, head of Yeerk security.

"Oh, calm down, Rachel," Tom said genially, giving her a "chill-out" wave. She had begun to morph to grizzly. "No need to go all hostile."

"Keep morphing, Rachel," I told her. "Ax?"

Ax moved quickly to Tom's side. His tail blade was against Tom's throat. Tom stood still. He made a mocking face, exaggerated fear.

"I'm alone, unarmed," Tom said, holding his arms up in surrender. "Hey, I'm morph-capable now, you know. If I wanted trouble I'd use this really cool jaguar morph I have."

"Let him go, Ax," I said.

Ax removed his tail but stayed within striking distance. A word from me and Tom's head would be rolling across the cave floor like a bowling ball.

"So, this is the whole team, huh?" Tom nodded. He shook his head ruefully. "Crazy cousin Rachel. I always knew you were too much for your own good."

<Shut up, Yeerk,> she said. <You're not my cousin. You're a snail living inside my cousin's head.>

"Snail? Oh, I'm wounded," the Yeerk inside Tom answered. "And there's Cassie. Marco. Your pet Andalite, of course. Hey, where's the bird?"

"How about we cut the crap?" I said.

"Absolutely, Killer." His eyes were cold, hostile. He was making no effort to pretend to actually be Tom. He knew that I knew what he was.

<Tom represents a faction of Yeerks who want some of what we want,> Arbron said.

"Some?"

"Yeah, some," Tom agreed. "Sorry, but we're not interested in hiding out in some out-of-the-way forest, some game preserve. That may be fine for the Taxxons. Me, I want something a little better than that. But then, I have even more to offer than Brother Arbron, here. You want the Pool ship? You want your mommy and daddy back, Big Jake the Yeerk Killer? You want this creature back?" He indicated his own body. "You want poor Tommy back? I can make all that happen."

I had to rein in a powerful desire to go after him. It's hard to conceive of the impotent rage you feel watching someone you love be reduced to a mindless puppet. "In exchange for what?"

"My people want it, too: the morphing power."

"You said you're already morph-capable."

"I am. And not just this body, by the way, but me. I've subjected my own true Yeerk self to the cube. You want to know what's funny? I can morph Tom. That's right, I can morph into my own host body. Cool, huh? But there are all these other Yeerks who are never going to get the chance to be free."

Marco snorted derisively. "Free? You don't want to be free."

Tom laughed. "Marco must be the one doing your thinking for you, Jake. You never were all that smart. You're right, Marco, I want something else. I want Visser One dead. I want the Council of Thirteen off my back. I want to lose the whole Empire. They're prisoners of their own tired old thinking. They can't see the future. We're a parasitic species, they can't see past that. We have the huge vulnerability of reliance on Kandrona rays. But morphed, permanently morphed, we won't need Kandrona rays, and we won't be parasites anymore. We can achieve a greater destiny."

He moved closer now. His fists were clenched at his side, his jaw seemed to tighten so that the words could barely force their way past bared teeth. I'd seen Tom this way once, just once, when he'd been wrongly accused of cheating on a test. It was as angry as Tom got, short of punching someone.

"Visser One is only capable of piling brute force on top of brute force. He's insane, you know. You can't rely on him! You can't hope for career advancement, to rise as you should. I should be a sub-visser by now, and in the small numbers. What I've done on this planet? I've been carrying him for the last three years. But as long as . . ." He stopped himself, forced a hard

smile. "Office politics. You don't want to hear about it."

"What do you want?" Marco asked him. "Give it to us A,B,C. What do you want?"

<Don't even listen to him,> Rachel growled. <We take him now, hold on to him for three days till the Yeerk starves to death. Then we have Tom back.>

Tom's Yeerk dropped the wise-guy attitude. He ignored Rachel and Marco and even Ax who still hovered close, twitching with readiness. "You take the Pool ship, Jake. You can keep it. But I get the Blade ship, and a hundred of my people, all treated with the morphing cube. And we get a free pass out of this system."

"And you take off to some far-off, unsuspecting planet, make victims of some other species?" Cassie cried.

"Hmm. Come to think of it, yes," Tom said. He waited. Grinned. "But . . ."

"Yeah?" I asked.

"But the Yeerk Empire will be gutted. Finished. I've told Visser One that I have information that the Andalite fleet is massing close by, using Jupiter as a shield to hide behind. So he's ordered most of our own fleet to stay in Zerospace, ready to emerge once the Andalites are committed. Not quite true. The Andalites are much closer than that."

That interested me. Interested me greatly, but could I believe him?

<Surely we cannot allow this creature to seize the Blade ship,> Ax said. <The Blade ship is a very powerful offensive weapon. As a warship it is even more dangerous than a Pool ship since it is as heavily armed and far faster and more maneuverable. We Andalites would have little to fear, but few other space-faring races could stand against such a ship.>

Tom's face smirked. "Little brother, you've got to know by now: Wars aren't won with clean hands."

"Don't listen to him," Cassie said, but it was almost a whisper.

"What do you have to offer?" I asked Tom.

"The keys to the kingdom, kid. I can give you the access codes for every system on the Pool ship. If you can take it, Brother Jake, you and your free Hork-Bajir and your new Taxxon allies, if you can take it, I can tell you how to fly it. Not only that, I have a plan to help you get aboard the Pool ship. And by the way, your old friend Visser One has temporarily transferred his headquarters to the Pool ship. The Pool ship and Visser One — that's game, set, and match." He grinned at me and said, "They'll carve your sanctimonious face up on Mount Rushmore, Jake-Boy. You'll be the savior of the human race."

"Thanks for the offer," I said. "I don't think so. Ax, take him. Rachel? Help Ax. Carefully!"

That rocked him for a second or two. Then he nodded. "I see: The Andalite's told you he can break security." He nodded. "He probably can, the Andalites are very good with computers. He'd have an hour before the codes shift. He would. Except that I've changed the code cycle to fifteen minutes." He glared at Ax. "Can you beat fifteen minutes, Andalite? Can you do that?"

CHAPTER 15

The keys were in my hands.

I could win. We could win.

If General Doubleday would provide the diversion. If the Taxxons would rally to us. If Tom's Yeerk provided us with the access codes. If Tom really could get us aboard the Pool ship and we could overpower the Yeerks still aboard. And if Ax could (and would) find a way to convince his people to ratify the promises we'd made to the Taxxons and Tom's dissident Yeerk faction.

Five "ifs." A lot. But at least now the number of "ifs" was a finite number.

A sixth "if": If Tom's Yeerk was telling the truth.

He had asked for no guarantees. Did he trust

me to keep my word? Would he risk everything on my word? True, he knew me through my brother's memories. And yet . . . and yet . . .

As we flew home, flew home impossibly free and alive after spending an hour with a few hundred Taxxons plus one of the highest ranking Yeerks, my mind was full of the details. Cassie left me alone for a while, but I knew she'd have something to say. I knew it. And I knew I had ignored her in the past at my own peril. I knew I should listen to her, trust her.

But I also knew what she'd say, and I didn't want to hear it. Just the same, after a while, as we flew in the dead night air above the wrecked town below, the waiting got to me.

<Cassie, just go ahead and say it,> I said finally.

<Say it? You're expecting some moral lecture from me about turning Tom's Yeerk and a hundred of his chosen people loose with a fantastically powerful warship to roam the galaxy? Never knowing what suffering he may inflict?>

<Something like that, yeah.>

<Because that's me, right? The voice of whining morality.>

She sounded bitter. I wasn't surprised. I was surprised by what came next.

<I gave the Yeerks the morphing cube,> she said. <Because of that the Taxxons may become a force for peace. And Tom, the real Tom, and

96

your parents, may be restored to us. And because of that, Tom's Yeerk has seen a way to betray his own people and become some kind of warlord on his own.>

I took a moment to digest that. She was actually blaming herself. <Cassie, these things happen. You can't always predict the results of the things you do. You try your best, take your best shot, and maybe it comes out right, and maybe it comes out . . . I don't know, confused.>

<Brilliant, isn't it? So I make the decisions, I make the big call, sanctimonious little me, I make the moral, optimistic decision, and where are we?>

<Better off than we were,> I said, but I was only half-listening now. An alarm bell was going off in my head. Why? What was the problem? What was it?

<And some species we don't know about is maybe doomed when a Blade ship full of morphing Yeerks descends on them.>

<It's never completely clean, Cassie. Doesn't work that way. But you try your best to keep it clean. The fact that you know you'll be dragged in the gutter doesn't mean you don't try like hell to stay out of it. You don't get a lot of straight-up good or evil choices. You get shades of gray. I mean, we started this war thinking we'd hold on till the great and glorious Andalites came to res-

cue us. Now we're making deals with Taxxons and Yeerks to gain a victory fast enough to keep the great and glorious Andalites from making their own shades-of-gray decision.>

<What are you going to do?> Cassie asked.

<I'm going to win,> I said. But I didn't believe it. Why? It was all there. It was all possible at least.

Of course Tom's Yeerk was lying in part. I was sure he was not interested in turning *nothlit,* that was a joke. The morphing cube was almost surely on board the Blade ship, and the Blade ship had its own small Yeerk pool facility. So of course he was lying about that.

But just as surely, he was telling the truth about wanting to seize the Blade ship and go into business for himself.

Tom. The Yeerk in his head. Had to believe him, after all, he'd known where we were, he obviously knew about Arbron, he could very easily have called in every Hork-Bajir-Controller on the planet and taken us down.

He'd had us right in the palm of his hand, and let us go. Had to trust that. Didn't I?

Yeah. But why did he trust me? Why did he trust me?

Trust breeds trust, right? Tom's Yeerk had shown he could be trusted, so he trusted us in return? Trusted me to get him all he wanted, all I'd agreed to?

No. No, that wasn't it. Tom's Yeerk wanted us to believe we could trust him. He didn't ask for assurances or cross-examine me because he didn't want me doing the same to him.

Then I saw it: Of course. I'd been looking at nothing but tactics; I'd overlooked emotion. The emotion of a vengeful Yeerk. He despised Visser One for being a failure, for being a brute, for refusing to promote him. "As long as . . ." Tom had started to say.

Yes. Visser One was not the only person Tom's Yeerk hated. Someone else was to blame for forcing this choice on an ambitious Yeerk.

Me. My friends. We were responsible for forcing this choice on Tom's Yeerk. In frustrating Visser One we had doomed Tom's Yeerk.

That was why Tom's Yeerk didn't ask for reassurances from us. He expected us to be dead. He would kill Visser One and us and sail off across the galaxy in the Blade ship with the morphing cube in his hands.

It came to me all at once that I could beat him. Use him and beat him.

One of those rare, perfect moments when a dozen nagging questions, an infinity of details, simply fall perfectly into place and form a single clear picture.

It took my breath away. The perfection of it. The pure, ruthless perfection of it.

All I had to do was send my friends to die.

Cassie was still talking to me, but I didn't hear her words. I had seen the vision. I could see the pure, straight line from point A to point Z.

I said, <Marco? Find the Chee. Find them. Bring Erek to me.>

<How am I going to do that?> Marco groused. <The Chee hideout is in the blast area. I tried, but it's nothing but destruction, you can't even tell where the streets used to be. And it's crawling with Yeerks shooting anything that moves. It would be very easy to get myself killed going back there.>

<Yeah, I know. Do it anyway,> I said. <I need the Chee.> I felt sick inside. High and low at once. Exalted. Twisted.

What chance was there that Marco would succeed? What chance that he would survive?

And worse in store for Rachel. I needed Tobias, and could not risk losing Ax. Cassie? No. It had to be Rachel. Only she would do it, could do it.

I had a few small changes to make to Tom's plan. The orders came easily, automatically as I dispatched my friends, one after the other. Only Rachel remained.

<Rachel, I have a job for you.>

I explained what I wanted her to do.

<You're sure, Jake?> she asked solemnly when I had finished. <Because if you tell me "Go!" I'll follow your orders. You know what that means.>

<Yeah, Rachel, I know what it means.>

Still she hesitated. <It won't be the Yeerk, Jake. It'll be Tom. It'll be him.>

<I know that,> I said. <And I . . . if it happens, if it comes down that way, I don't have a plan for getting you out. You'd be on your own.>

<That's how I like it.>

<Okay, then. Get started. Make sure Cassie doesn't know.>

<You still don't trust her?> Rachel said angrily.

<She loves us both, Rachel,> I said. <I can't make her part of this. I can't let her know in advance, so, you know, if it happens, if it happens, I don't want her spending the rest of her life wondering if she could have stopped it somehow.>

Rachel said, <Okay, Jake. You're right. And you're right to use me for this. Not exactly something I'm proud of, maybe, but later, you know, if — don't be blaming yourself, okay?>

She angled her eagle's wings to take the wind, and flew away.

The plan was a fragile thing in my mind, a

construct of if-then possibilities, of hopes, optimism, and cynicism in equal measure.

I would use everyone, put everyone in harm's
way. And I knew — knew beyond any doubt —
that someone, and maybe more than someone, I
loved was going to die.

CHAPTER 16

It took all day to get my chess pieces in place. The hardest one was Erek the Chee.

Marco found him. He found him after twice being spotted and shot by Yeerk forces. But it's hard to kill an Animorph. A wounded morph has only to demorph to be reconstituted as a whole human.

Of course a dead morph is a dead Animorph, and Marco came very close to not making it.

He was not happy by the time he dragged into camp late in the day. I had almost given up hope.

Erek is a Chee, one of a race of sentient robots created millennia ago by the Pemalites. The Pemalites were gentle, wise, intelligent creatures who were obliterated by the Howlers long, long

ago. The Pemalites believed in peace. And the Chee they created, despite being unimaginably powerful and equipped with formidable holographic technology, were incapable of violence.

This was not to say that the Chee didn't have a side in the war. They were our allies. They were the ultimate spies, able to pass as humans, as they had since arriving on Earth as refugees back in the days of the pharaohs of Egypt.

The Chee had spied for us, hoped we would win, but they would not help us kill. They couldn't help or cause anyone to kill or even to be hurt. I counted on that.

Erek smiled at me with a human face that should belong to a guy my own age. Of course beneath the hologram was a machine that looked as though it was built of stainless steel and ivory, like a stylized dog walking erect.

"Jake, I'm pleased to see you still alive," Erek said. "Pleased to see all of you."

"And we're relieved to see you, Erek. How are the Chee doing?"

He shrugged. "Well, our house is gone. But the underground facility is intact. All our people are safe. We've been through worse in five thousand years among your lovely people. I mean, I survived the Huns and they were quite unpleasant. The dogs are safe at least."

The Chee carried on their master's love of canine forms. They took in stray or lost dogs whenever they could.

"Erek, we need your help."

"Always glad to help, within the limits of my programming," he answered cautiously.

"We're taking the Pool ship," I said.

He hesitated, thought that over. "I don't see how I'm going to be able to help you. We don't have a lot of data on the Pool ship. Nothing you don't already know."

"It's not information we need," I said. "We need your skills. We need your active participation. We need you there."

His eyes grew dark, a holographic but very real-seeming reaction. "I can't do that, Jake. We both know there'll be fighting. I can't be part of that."

I took a deep breath, not wanting to say what I was about to say. "Here's the thing, Erek, I know what you can and can't do. So I'm going to use that to force your hand. I'm sorry. But we're down to it, now. We're right down to it."

"What are you planning?" He switched off the "Erek" holographic facade and revealed his true self. Maybe that was to intimidate me. Maybe it was just a way of conveying anger.

"We know you can't fight us. So we're going to take you, carry you if we have to, put you in a position where you'll cooperate because refusing

to cooperate will force us to take lives. Your refusal to cooperate would be the trigger for killing.

"Ax? Bring your prisoner."

I had dispatched Ax and Cassie to take a prisoner, a known Controller, a human-Controller. Chapman.

And he was not happy.

"Ax, if I tell you to kill this Controller, will you do it?" I asked him.

<Yes,> Ax answered truthfully. <He is a ranking Yeerk, an enemy who has done great damage to human freedom.>

"This is low," Erek grated. "This is so far beneath you, Jake."

Weird blackmailing a creature you know is physically capable of obliterating you down to your individual molecules. Weird trusting that he won't, can't, do any such thing.

"Sorry," I said again. "But we'll keep you in a position where every time you refuse to help, we take a life. And I'll make you this promise: Your help will minimize the casualties."

Erek said a long string of words I didn't understand.

"What?"

"I was offering you my opinion of your morals and your ethics and your sense of decency," Erek spat. "I was speaking an ancient Mesopotamian dialect known for its wide variety of curse words."

I nodded. "Tell you the truth, Erek, your being mad at me is the least of my problems. Marco? Erek is your property. He tries to leave, stop him. If he succeeds in leaving, Ax, you'll execute this Controller."

I shot a challenging, defensive look at Cassie. "Any comment?"

"No."

I glared at my friends, all of whom were looking somber. Erek had been with us, an ally, a friend, for a long time. "Does anyone have anything to say?"

No one did.

"Good. Now, Ax? In addition to keeping an eye on our friend, here, it's time for you to phone the Andalite fleet. You tell them you succeeded in stopping our raid on the Yeerk pool. Tell them the Yeerks are all here on Earth like sitting ducks. But they can't strike yet because you, *aristh* Aximili, are going to deliver a major Yeerk warship right into their laps. You're going to hand them an entire, intact Pool ship."

<You are asking me to lie to my people,> Ax said. <The Yeerks have stopped concentrating forces on Earth. They are awaiting the construction of a new Yeerk pool.>

"I'm not asking you to lie to your people, Ax. I'm *telling* you to. We need them close enough to be of use, but we also need to give them a reason

not to start blasting away at Earth. Call the Andalite fleet. Tell them what I've told you to tell them. I'm your prince, Ax: Do it."

I didn't wait to hear his answer. I knew it. Or thought I did.

James and his people came flying in, landed and demorphed. "You called?"

It's always disturbing for me seeing the auxiliary Animorphs demorphed. When we still had the morphing cube we decided to add some members. But it's impossibly complicated and time-consuming to make sure each and every person is Yeerk-free. So we figured out who the Yeerks would have never infested, who they would have overlooked: the handicapped. Plenty of fully functional human hosts around, why hassle with all the drawbacks of dealing with a handicap?

We knew handicapped kids would be Yeerk-free. We also knew they'd be even more willing than most people to accept a treatment that would allow them physical freedom in animal form.

We'd used them. And now they lay there rather than standing because for the most part they couldn't stand. Or, if they could stand, they couldn't see.

"Yeah, James. We need all your people. As you know, we're going after the Pool ship."

"Yes, I know."

"It's going to be as dangerous as it gets, and I have a very tough assignment for you."

"Okay, well, you know I'm in. But I'll need to talk to the others, see how they feel. I think some of them will want to sit this one out. I mean, after losing Ray . . . I mean, Jake, some of the young ones, you know, some of them are having —"

"James, we didn't give them morphing power so they could have fun flying around. This is when we need them. All of them. You understand? You've taken on the role as their leader, so lead: I want them all. Every last one."

"Jake, some of these kids, I mean, they're all their families have, you know? They're still just starting to deal with Ray's death. It's not like we haven't fought. I can't . . ."

"Look, if we lose this battle it's over, you understand me?!" I raised my voice to be heard by everyone. "If we lose it's over. This is the battle. This is the last stand. We lose and here's what happens: The Yeerk fleet fights the Andalite fleet. If the Yeerks win they'll be free to enslave every living human being and kill the ones they don't want. If the Andalites win there's a very good chance they'll sterilize Earth: kill everything in order to end the Yeerk menace once and for all. So, you don't like me telling you what to do, you don't like your job, you don't like me, period? I

don't really care. Before this night is over the casualties will be piled high and some of you standing here right now will be dead and I don't care because we are going to win. Is that clear? We're taking that Pool ship and before this night is over we'll have Visser One right here." I held up my tight-clenched fist.

I was ranting. I was trembling. I'd never done this before. Never put myself forward as some kind of Napoleon wannabe. I felt like a jerk. Like some kind of nut. My friends must have thought I'd lost my mind. But no one said so.

No one but Marco. "You know, you're turning into Rachel." He frowned. "Where is she, anyway?"

CHAPTER 17

I was in falcon morph, floating high, high in the air, rising on the updraft of warmth that still came from the smoldering ashes of the center of town. Usually night is a bad time for a peregrine. Night air is cold air and cold air is dead air. But flying above the black destruction I had all the lift I needed.

I could see the Pool ship, still resting beside the crater that had once been the Yeerk pool. Could they see me, Visser One and his Yeerks? They could if they tried. I wasn't invisible. But they didn't attack, didn't send a Bug fighter up to Dracon me.

Why not? Maybe Tom's Yeerk wasn't ready to kill me, yet.

Or Maybe Visser One saw me, knew what I

was, and waited, like the spider in his web watching the fly. He wanted me to come to him. He wanted me as badly as I wanted him.

Careful what you wish for, Visser.

Careful what you wish for, Jake.

I had visited General Doubleday. He was as shaken up as anyone I've ever seen, but determined.

He'd followed our suggestion, reluctantly at first. He'd locked away as many of his men as he could. It was ten hours till the first Controller reached the point where he couldn't hold out any longer. He made a break for it.

"What did you do?" I had asked him.

"We warned him once. Gave him a direct order. Then the MP shot him."

"That must have been tough," I'd said.

"The MP aimed for a leg shot, but the private slipped. Bullet caught him in the head." The general held out an empty bottle and showed it to me. "This thing crawled out of the man's head. Crawled out through the bullet hole."

A Yeerk lay writhing in the bottle.

"There's your enemy, General," I'd said.

Some of the Controllers had tried to work together to rush the door. Others had waited as long as they could. Seventeen percent of the general's men had been infested. But now he had a strike force of almost a thousand men, Yeerk-free. Yeerk-free, and, having seen the enemy close-at-hand, they were motivated.

I'd given him all the details I safely could.

"They may come after you with Bug fighters — that would be the best we could hope for. The greater likelihood is that either the Pool ship or the Blade ship will attack you directly."

"I've got what amounts to a scratch battalion, a few tanks, a few helicopter gunships. I've seen those Bug fighters in action. My men will fight, but they can't win."

"That's right, General, they can't," I said. "But if they'll fight, keep up the diversion, we can win. I have about a dozen of my people coming to join you. They'll be right out front."

"With all due respect to your people, son, they may be great in hand-to-hand combat, but you're guerrilla fighters by nature. Your abilities are geared for that kind of warfare. You're asking me for a good, old-fashioned cavalry charge, here. You're asking me for the Charge of the Light Brigade."

"We need the diversion," I said. "Visser One has to believe the Yeerk traitor is telling him the truth. So you have to attack, but once the Yeerks come after you all you can do is dig in and take cover. The Yeerks only have one way of fighting:

Attack with everything they've got. They'll go right after you. Visser One doesn't know tactics; he fights with a sledgehammer."

"If you've got a big enough sledgehammer that's all you need, son."

I was hearing those weary, wry words as I flew above the Pool ship. It was a monstrous thing. Bigger than an aircraft carrier. More powerful than all the forces of humankind combined and multiplied a hundredfold. The Dracon cannon on the Pool ship could burn a hole through an asteroid.

But it was a sledgehammer, a great, lumbering beast designed for war in the weightlessness of space. And, anyway, if we succeeded it would be our sledgehammer.

I saw movement below. Hork-Bajir patrols. A pair of Bug fighters flying a loose figure eight low above the desolation.

Closer in to the Pool ship the Hork-Bajir patrols increased till they formed a solid, shoulder-to-shoulder ring around the ship. Hork-Bajir and human-Controller snipers stood atop the engine pods. Visser One was taking no chances with his crown jewels.

I wondered what time it was. No way to carry a watch, obviously, and I could no longer spot bank clocks. They'd all been destroyed.

I floated and waited. Floated and waited and went over my plan again and again. I could see holes in it now. I could see nothing but holes. It would never work. It would never work.

I saw movement down below. A pair of Humvees approaching an outer ring checkpoint, headlights playing on wrecked, charred brick walls and burned out cars. Hork-Bajir- and human-Controller guards checked ID's and passed them through.

Now I didn't need a clock. It was go time.

I swooped down, diving faster and faster, matching speed with the Humvees. I dropped through the gaping window of a blackened home and out through the far side. That would throw off any sensors that might be tracking me.

I used all my falcon speed and aimed for the bouncing rear window of the second Humvee. I swooped through, landed hard with a bounce against the seat back.

A human-Controller I didn't know was driving. Tom was in the passenger seat. He turned to look at me.

"Very unsettling when you do that," he said.

<Good,> I answered.

Cassie appeared to be lying on the backseat, handcuffed, ankles bound, a Hork-Bajir sitting beside her with a Dracon weapon leveled at her head.

Her face was bruised. One eye swollen almost shut. There were bloody cuts on her arms. Her morphing suit was in shreds.

"Gotta hand it to your girl back there," Tom said nonchalantly. "She takes a beating pretty well. Hope I didn't get carried away, Jake-boy, but it isn't every day I get a chance to pound on an Animorph. She didn't cry, didn't say a word. Almost took the fun out of it."

<Shut up, you Yeerk scum,> I snapped. <I have to do business with you, but don't push your luck. Cassie. Cassie, are you okay?>

No answer. I didn't expect one.

"Bruised my fists," Tom's Yeerk said, displaying his hand.

<I said, shut up.>

"Whatever. Time to get small, Killer Jake. Security up ahead there."

I demorphed, made a point of stroking the apparent wounds, made another angry remark to Tom's Yeerk for verisimilitude, then went fly. Back in morph I used private thought-speak, audible to only one person. <Rachel?>

<I'm here, Jake.>

I zoomed around and then headed for Cassie's bruised, battered face.

As I approached a landing, her swollen eye opened slightly. My compound eyes saw a hundred fragmented images of an eye opening.

And of the steel-and-ivory machine beneath the hologram.

CHAPTER 18

The Humvees approached the wall-to-wall line of Hork-Bajir around the Pool ship and came to a stop.

A Hork-Bajir- and a human-Controller stepped over to the window like cops getting ready to hand out tickets.

They spotted Tom, and I could hear the formal stiffness in their voices. "Sir, you understand we still need to conduct a thorough search and check your identity."

"You'd better," Tom snarled. "Lax security makes me cranky."

The human-Controller shined a powerful light around the inside of the vehicle. He introduced a sensor probe that to my fly senses registered as a

117

fantastical wizard's wand. I could see energy radiating in wild colors, invisible most likely to human eyes.

"I only read two complex life-forms," the guard said. "I'm showing several insect readings, but only two complex life-forms: yours, sir, and the driver's. The prisoner is not registering as a life-form."

It was already going bad. What was this new sensor? We'd never seen this instrument before. I tensed, ready to leap free and demorph. But in the enclosed space of the Humvee we were trapped, helpless. We wouldn't be able to bring our force to bear.

Tom said, "Well, as much as I respect your new toy there, I count three: one, two, three."

"Yes, sir."

"You can count to three, right?"

"Yes, sir."

"Do you know what that prisoner is? That's an Animorph. You think maybe Visser One would like to see her just as soon as possible?"

"Yes, sir!"

"As for the insect life-forms, they're endemic to this planet. But I'll be sure to use the Gleet BioFilter before I enter the ship."

The guard must have been satisfied because moments later we were on the move. I rested calmly on a titanium rod that, to me, seemed as thick as an oak tree.

No one said anything for a while, and I could see very little with my limited fly senses.

Then, in a calm, low-pitched voice, Tom said, "How's it going, little brother? You still there?"

<I'm still here,> I said.

"Good, glad to hear it. And all your little friends are there with you?"

<Shut up, Yeerk,> I snapped. <We work together because we have to. We don't make small talk.>

Tom's Yeerk laughed. "Oh, you're a surly bunch, aren't you? No one talks to me. No one but Rachel, who told me to . . . well, you can guess what Rachel told me to do."

<Whatever she said goes for all of us,> I answered.

"Surly and unpleasant. Oh, well. Time to go see the visser. My plan is working perfectly, don't you think?"

Tom thought Cassie was real. And he thought all of us were hiding out somewhere on her body. His plan was working fine. Ours was working even better.

Another delay. And then, at last, I heard that thought-speak voice.

Visser One.

<What have we here?>

"One of the Animorphs, Visser. My people captured her and questioned her. Questioned her . . . forcefully."

<So I see. Congratulations.> He sounded almost annoyed, like he wasn't all that happy to see Tom succeed where he had failed. <Have you passed through the Gleet BioFilter? I don't want any surprises.>

"Yes, Visser, of course," Tom's Yeerk lied. The Gleet BioFilter detects and eliminates nonprimary life-forms — anything "riding" on a human or Hork-Bajir body.

<One of the so-called Animorphs. This one would be . . . Cassie, yes?>

Now I could see him, a mosaic of him, in my compound eyes. He loomed close, leering down with his mouthless Andalite face, stalk eyes widening out.

Suddenly his tail whipped around and delivered a slapping blow. Fast. So fast that even my fly reflexes would not have saved me. But of course the blow never reached me. It was stopped by force fields that overlapped the hologram. Just as Tom's torturing blows had been.

<I would kill her myself,> Visser One grated. <The trouble these creatures have caused me.>

"Perhaps not just yet, Visser," Tom demurred. "She may still be useful as bait. Why not hold her and hand her over to some worthy, loyal Yeerk as a host body?"

<They are hard to hold on to,> Visser One said. <If you even appear to be thinking of morphing you'll die, Animorph. Of course, you're likely to die either way.>

"Cassie" said nothing.

<But pleasure can wait,> Visser One said. <Report what you have learned.>

Tom clasped his hands behind his back and assumed a respectful but casual stance. "The Animorphs' leader has made contact with human military forces. A combined force of human soldiers and Animorphs will attack very soon. The goal will be to use the attack as a diversion, to allow the Animorphs to infiltrate this ship."

Visser One laughed. <They would try to take a Pool ship? Are they such fools?>

"Don't forget, they have an Andalite among them. They would use his skills to break our security codes. And there is more, Visser."

<More? What more?>

"I . . . I'm not certain, Visser, but I believe my people may have penetrated a second conspiracy, every bit as dangerous."

<Tell me of —>

"Visser!" A new voice. Human. I vaguely perceived a human-Controller, a woman.

<You interrupt me?>

"With your permission, Visser, this may be the report I've been waiting for," Tom said smoothly.

"Visser . . . I apologize for interrupting," the woman said, "but a party of Hork-Bajir have arrived at the perimeter with a Taxxon prisoner."

<A Taxxon prisoner? If some Taxxon is giving trouble, kill it, don't waste my time with disciplinary matters like this.>

Tom intervened again. "I believe this is a very special Taxxon, Visser. You may choose to hear what he has to say."

Moments later the Taxxon, accompanied by Hork-Bajir guards, shuffled and writhed into the room. He was a hundred great worms in my compound eyes. But the colors were different. I saw the red jelly eyes as an almost psychedelic violet.

<Well?> Visser One demanded. <I'm not a patient Yeerk, explain the great mystery here.>

Tom proceeded to explain his penetration of a Taxxon alliance with the Animorphs. The Taxxon, straining to form coherent speech with its inadequate mouthparts, confirmed the tale.

"In a matter of moments now, Visser, this three-part attack will take place. Human soldiers will attack, the Taxxons will destroy the unfinished Yeerk pool, and the Animorphs themselves will use the confusion to attempt to penetrate this ship."

Visser One nodded. But was there hesitation

in his bleary-looking Andalite eyes? No genius, maybe, Visser One, but he had an instinct for survival. He was moving back and forth, pacing, hooves clicking on the deck, stalk eyes wandering randomly.

Tom said, "If we move swiftly, we will destroy all our foes in one swoop. The Pool ship and its Bug fighters can quickly eliminate the human soldiers, and simply by lifting off we can doom the Animorph attempt at infiltration."

<And what of these treasonous Taxxons?>

"They must be stopped quickly but carefully: We don't want to damage the new Yeerk pool. I respectfully suggest, Visser, that I take temporary command of your Blade ship and deal with the Taxxons personally. Never fear: I will kill only as many as I need to, and drive the rest back to their labor."

So, here it is, I thought. *The moment of truth. The Visser would buy it or not.* The silence stretched on. Too long.

Visser One had smelled the rat.

<I don't like so much good luck,> Visser One hissed. <I've fought to seize this planet for years. For years! And suddenly now everything falls into my hands? I don't trust good luck. For all I know, this Animorph, this Cassie creature, has managed to carry her fellow bandits in with her.>

"But, Visser, the Gleet BioFilter . . ."

<They've beaten the filter before,> Visser One shouted. <No! No! There's something wrong here, something very wrong. . . . Look how she stands there, beaten, whipped, cowed. No, it's too easy. And this Taxxon, how can I be sure he, too, isn't one of them? They can take any shape. How can I be sure?>

"Very simply," Tom said calmly. "Order the Taxxon to eat the Animorph girl. If the Taxxon is an Animorph in morph, he will refuse. If not, then the girl — and any hidden morphs concealed on her person — will be consumed. Thus, we will be sure of both."

<Yes!> Visser One cried. <Guards, watch every corner of this room, shoot anything that moves, do you hear me? Anything! Don't wait for orders. If they're here they'll try to demorph and remorph. Shoot anything! And now, hungry brother Taxxon: If you are a true Taxxon, rid us of this girl.>

The Taxxon did not hesitate. It reared up, opened its lamprey mouth, and slammed itself greedily down, teeth bared.

CHAPTER 19

"No! No!" Cassie cried. "Nooo!"

The Taxxon's mouth ripped Cassie apart, chewed arms and legs, spilled organs out onto the deck of the Pool ship, and finally lifted off her head in one fatal bite.

The voice — really very like Cassie's — screamed, cried, begged for mercy.

Tom waved good-bye. "If you are there by some chance, little brother Jake, bye-bye!"

I saw it all from inside the illusion, for illusion it was. "Cassie" was Erek, the Chee.

Tom had betrayed us, as I knew he would. He believed we were all hiding on the true Cassie. He believed he had beaten the true Cassie, and that she had submitted in order to make her capture seem real.

He believed he had now fed her, and me, and all of us, to the hunger-mad Taxxon.

But the Taxxon was no more a Taxxon than "Cassie" was the real Cassie.

Tobias in Taxxon morph gorged on an illusion. The Cassie hologram was a horror film directed by Erek. Bit by bit he replaced illusions of Cassie with illusions of empty space. Until, gory bit by gory bit, she was gone, consumed by the Taxxon who kept at it until not even a bloodstain was left on the ship's deck.

It would never have fooled a true Taxxon — even Chee holograms and force fields cannot project taste. But Tobias acted his part to perfection and the two Yeerks, Visser One and Tom, bought the performance entirely.

Erek, now visibly nothing but deck, rolled away, out of range of any sudden movement by Visser One that would reveal his presence.

<You did good, Erek,> I said.

He didn't answer. He couldn't. And in any case, I knew what his answer would be. I had left him no choice. Any failure on Erek's part would have been the trigger for my ordering a slaughter. Chee programming chose the less violent path.

<Very good,> Visser One said, laughing. <I've lived to see at least one of them die. That was

very satisfying. Now, go, my good and faithful servant: Take the Blade ship. Kill the Taxxon rebels for me! Hammer them into submission!>

"Yes, Visser," Tom said, barely able to conceal his glee.

He thought he had it all in his grasp, right then. His voice gave nothing away, but I knew the Yeerk inside my brother's head was triumphant. Ecstatic!

He had killed me. Killed all of us. And now, he would take possession of the Blade ship. Then, if my guess was right, he'd wait while Visser One annihilated General Doubleday's troops, and then, when Visser One was least expecting it, Tom's Yeerk would strike a surprise blow and destroy the Pool ship itself.

Tom's Yeerk would be left in command of the heavily armed and very fast Blade ship — almost surely the hiding place for the morphing cube. Tom's Yeerk would take his new command into Zero-space to reemerge far, far away with a hard core of loyal followers and the power to morph. He wouldn't have to stay behind to face the likely arrival of the Andalites. He would be safe and in control.

It was a neat plan. And if I had trusted him I'd be dead, along with all my friends.

<Tobias, you okay?> I said.

<I think I chipped a couple of Taxxon teeth

munching on Erek's force fields, but yeah, I'm good.>

<Marco? Cassie? Ax?> I called.

<We're all okay, Jake,> Marco reported. <The good thing is that at least this flea morph I'm in has no interest in sucking Taxxon blood.>

<Still no sign of Rachel,> Cassie said. <I thought you said she would join us.>

<I'm sure she's okay,> I said. <Rachel takes care of herself. Now, you guys get to work. We need navigation control, and we need it as soon as possible.>

Marco said, <Do you think we should even try the codes Tom gave us?>

Ax answered for me. <Since he has, as predicted, betrayed us, it is likely the so-called codes he gave us are not only useless, but may well be self-destruct codes.>

<Ax is right,> I said. <You guys have to do it the hard way. Get going.>

Visser One helped us out inadvertently by ordering the Hork-Bajir guards to <Take that filthy Taxxon out and eliminate him. He'll give you no trouble now that he's been well fed!>

The Hork-Bajir led the Taxxon away. But neither Tobias, nor my friends hiding on his morphed form, had any reason to fear. The Hork-Bajir guards were Toby and twelve of her people.

My brother left the bridge of the Pool ship. He

would be taken by Bug fighter up to the Blade ship in orbit.

The Pool ship lifted off, a slight vibration being the only evidence. Off the earth to the safety of the skies, or so Visser One believed.

Five Animorphs, twelve free Hork-Bajir, and one Chee were now aboard the Pool ship, unsuspected. The plan was on track.

<Doing good, huh, Jake?> Rachel said, her thought-speak voice already fading with distance.

I couldn't answer.

CHAPTER 20

The Pool ship rose from the earth, bigger than anything human eyes had beheld in the skies. Up and up, but not so high yet.

I could see little of the room with my limited senses. Impossible to understand large spaces with fly eyes. So I searched out relative darkness. I searched out a space where the air motion was minimal. I had used the fly morph many times before and I was good at interpreting the fractured data of its senses.

I landed upside down on an almost horizontal surface and hung there for a moment, trying to assemble a picture of the Pool ship's battle bridge.

It seemed to be an oval in shape, though I

couldn't be sure. There were dozens of Controllers, mostly Hork-Bajir, with a scattering of humans. They sat or stood before glowing display screens. Others stood at attention, awaiting the visser's orders.

The visser paced back and forth, nervous or just feeling a rush of anticipation, I couldn't guess which.

"There, Visser!" a human voice sang out. "Human military forces on the move."

<On main screen,> Visser One ordered. <Magnify.>

"We have a preliminary estimate. Seven hundred and nine humans. Twelve of the tracked ground vehicles the humans call tanks, Visser. Nineteen rotary wing vehicles. Threat analysis: minimal."

I could see the main view screen. It was upside down from my perspective, and a dizzying array of weirdly distorted colors, but I could make it out. I could see what Visser One could see: General Doubleday's forces, moving forward through the burned debris below, still moving forward, following orders, despite the fact that their target, their objective, the Pool ship now hovered a thousand feet over their heads.

A Hork-Bajir voice jumped in. "They were deployed to attack us on the ground, Visser. They seem at a loss."

<Brilliant insight,> the visser said with acid sarcasm.

"Now showing fixed wing aircraft on approach," another human voice said calmly. "Nine total."

"Visser, I recommend allowing the Bug fighters to take out the aircraft. We can use our Dracon cannon on widest possible dispersion and destroy all the ground forces with a single sustained shot."

<Yes,> Visser One said. Then, sounding almost regretful at being cheated of a real battle, he said, <Simple creatures. Did they really imagine they would accomplish anything?>

Where were Erek and Ax? Surely it had been long enough. Surely the Chee had penetrated Yeerk security by now. We should have control of navigation. I didn't want to bother them, they were surely doing their best. But neither could I watch wholesale slaughter of the troops on the ground and do nothing.

"Dracon cannon configured, Visser. Permission to fire?"

If they fired the main Dracon cannon on widest dispersion it would not kill the men on the ground quickly. It would kill them slowly. They would cook. They would grow warmer and warmer, as the diluted Dracon energy heated them up. Hotter. Hotter till some began to pass out. Others would go crazy as their brains fried. And then the men, those already dead and those who still clung to life, would burn.

"Visser!"

<Yes, what is it?>

"Visser . . . the display . . . I believe there are morphs down there with the attacking human troops."

The viewscreen veered wildly, rushing in for a close-up like someone taking home video.

I clearly saw a lioness loping along, a squad of soldiers hurrying beside it, weapons at the ready. I could see faces as they looked up fearfully at the Pool ship. Some stopped to fire up at us.

Another morph, a rhino came lumbering into view. It was comical. Pitiful. Men with guns and a handful of fugitives from a zoo trying to attack a ship that could blow asteroids out of the sky.

<The rest of the Animorphs!> the visser cried gleefully. <Hah hah hah! I guess they're having a hard time infiltrating my ship, eh?>

Nervous, toadying laughter all around. Someone reported that Tom had reached the Blade ship. The Blade ship was reporting readiness to join the attack.

<Yes, yes, tell him to go deal with the Taxxons. This, however, is all mine,> Visser One crowed. Then, in a much different tone, almost wistful,

<How long I have waited for this moment. The bandits out in the open, targeted, on-screen, unable to escape . . .>

"Permission to fire Dracon cannon?"

<No, no, cancel wide dispersion,> the visser ordered. <I want to see them burn, one by one. Move us in. Use narrow beam. Forget the human soldiers, they're irrelevant. Rid me of these Animorphs, one by one. Close-up! Maximum magnification. Let me see them die!>

I couldn't be patient any longer. <Ax? Marco? What is keeping you?> I cried.

<Had a fight,> Marco answered. I could hear the pain in his thought-speak voice.

At that same moment a new report reached the bridge. "Visser! Casualties in engineering!" a Hork-Bajir voice said.

<What is it? Another plasma explosion?> Visser One asked.

"No, Visser, all engines are nominal. All systems are nominal."

<Well, find out what's happened down there then,> Visser One said, sounding petulant rather than concerned. <Now target the morphs. Begin firing.>

"Firing," the neutral voice reported.

The shot caught the hindquarters of the rhinoceros. For a horrifying moment the front legs kept running. The creature — a girl named Tricia — toppled forward, dug its horn into the dirt, rolled over, and was dead.

<Hah hah! Good shot! They burn well, these Animorphs!>

I felt sick inside. I should do something. I should stop this. That was the auxiliary Animorphs down there on the ground dying. Burning.

<No, no, you have to lead them a bit. Look! You can get two at . . . good shot!>

<Marco,> I pleaded. <Marco, they're killing James's people.>

<Erek's doing his best, so is Ax,> Marco answered.

<How long?>

A moment's pause while Marco queried the Chee and the Andalite.

<Three minutes,> he said at last.

It was a death sentence. Three minutes. More than enough time for the sharpshooters on the bridge. Too much time.

They fired.

If I demorphed here I'd be seen. Nowhere to hide. I'd be shot. Killed. Accomplish nothing.

Couldn't die. I was in charge. It was my plan. No time for gestures. Win, that was all I had to do: Win.

Visser One said, <Look, it's trying to repair itself by demorphing. Get it now! No, fool! There. Yes!>

"We're taking fire, Visser. The fixed wing air-craft have launched missiles."

<Destroy them,> Visser One said, too distracted by the murder of Animorphs to care overly much about minor matters.

The Hork-Bajir voice spoke again. "Confirm casualties in engineering, Visser. One Hork-Bajir. He appears to have suffered some sort of animal attack."

That news made the visser sit up and listen. He spun his stalk eyes around to the speaker. <What?>

I used the moment to push off and swoop down. I landed between his stalk eyes. Ax had admitted it was one of the very few spots on an Andalite's body that he cannot easily see. I rested very still on Visser One's head. The stalks were like snakes to me, impossibly thick, but flexible, bending this way and that, high over my head. The eyes floated up there, glaring daggers at the Hork-Bajir crewman.

<*Animal* attack?> Visser One grated.

Then, another human-Controller reported in, "Visser, we've contacted engineering and they are responding that everything is normal. The wounded Hork-Bajir was a disciplinary matter."

Of course: Someone down in engineering, one of my friends, had morphed and was now passing as a Yeerk crew member.

<Don't bother me with any more disciplinary matters,> Visser One said. <There! Look! Another morph! Get it! Get it!>

<Marco!> I yelled. <It's now or never!>

<You missed! No, wait, there, he burns! He burns!>

"Visser, that appears to be the last of the morphs."

<Ah, well, all good things must end,> Visser One said. <But it was a good ending. Be sure to save the recorded data — I will wish to play that scene over and over again. Now, set Dracon cannon for wide dispersal, let's end this game.>

"Dracon cannon configured, Visser."

<Fire.>

"Firing."

<Ah, the humans have begun to notice, eh? Ah hah hah! Look how they squirm!>

"They will suffer one hundred percent casualties in thirty seconds."

<Marco!> I cried.

<Got it!> he answered.

<Then do it! Now!>

<They burn, they burn!> the visser exulted.

Finally, "Visser, the helm is not answering."

<What do you mean the helm is not answering? We're drifting off-target! Get us back over the target!>

"Helm is unresponsive, Visser!"

137

He bounded over to the helmsman's position and seized the controls himself. I had a perfect view. <Engineering! That fool in engineering must have . . .>

I could practically see the wheels turning in his brain. I could almost see the thought process, as one by one the clues fell into place.

<They are on board!> Visser One said, aghast. <They're here. They're on board! They sacrificed the girl and used her as a Trojan horse!>

He still hadn't quite gotten it, but he was getting there. He still had not figured out that Tom had betrayed him.

"Visser, we appear to be heading toward a low orbit."

<I can see that!> Visser One raged. <Do we still have communications?>

"Yes."

<Then raise the Blade ship. Order it to approach. If necessary it can fire to disable our engines.>

It was almost too perfect. Visser One was actually going to invite Tom to approach. He was all but sealing his own doom.

<I want every Hork-Bajir who can stand to meet me outside engineering,> Visser One said.

He was trembling, I could feel it so clearly. I savored his fear and rage. I had watched, helpless, while he murdered James and his people. Watched while he gloated.

Now I wanted him to feel afraid.

<This ends now,> Visser One said harshly.

And silently I replied, *Yes, it does.*

CHAPTER 21

I hunkered down and held on as Visser One raced through the Pool ship. Hork-Bajir flocked to him, fell into step behind him. Down gloomy hallways, across open, hangarlike spaces, and then cramming into seemingly endless stair-wells. Descending, always descending.

<Marco! Cassie! We're on our way down there. Visser One and a whole bunch of his people.>

I was beginning to understand why it had taken Marco, Cassie, Tobias, Ax, and Erek so long. Engineering was quite a distance from the bridge.

Three corridors converged together at a pair

of wide blast doors. Hork-Bajir- and human-Controllers pressed close together.

<Dracon weapons on medium power,> Visser One ordered. <When the door opens begin firing. Fire until your power cells run dry, do you understand me?>

"Visser, there are surely some of our own people still alive in —"

The visser spun, whipped his Andalite tail, and decapitated the Hork-Bajir who had interrupted him.

<Medium power won't damage the machinery but it will kill every living thing in there! You! All of you, form three rows right here. First row of Hork-Bajir kneels, second row of humans stands, third row of Hork-Bajir fires above the heads of row two. Am I clear?>

He was clear. And if he wasn't, no one was going to say anything.

I spotted Toby, recognizable only by virtue of the fact that she was a bit shorter than the average Hork-Bajir female. Presumably her companions were in the crowd as well.

I called to my friends. <Hey, guys, they're going to fire blind. They'll saturate the room with Dracon beams on medium setting, kill everything. Are you ready?>

<Yep. We're good,> Marco reported.

I launched, flew down and away, zipping through rapidly shuffling legs. The visser's troops were forming up, strangely reminiscent of the kind of array you'd have seen in the Revolutionary War. They might as well have been redcoats ready to fire volleys.

<Open the doors,> Visser One ordered.

The blast doors slid open on the main engineering station, a semicircle not so different from the bridge itself. But the room was on a vastly larger scale, as much as ten stories tall, dominated by three huge pillars of something that looked like glowing red clay.

The instant the doors opened the three close-packed ranks of Hork-Bajir and humans began firing. They poured energy into that room. There were cries from Hork-Bajir, humans, and Taxxons within, quickly silenced.

<Keep firing!> Visser One urged. <Assault teams ready. As soon as I order the firing to stop, rush the room!>

I flew away from the scene, propelled by a tail wind of hot air coming from the oven that was engineering.

Down a corridor, left down a side hall.

<In here,> Ax said. A small door slid open.

I zoomed through and the door slid shut behind me. I demorphed and stood facing Ax, Marco, Cassie, and Tobias.

"Well, Jake," Marco said cheerily. "Imagine meeting you here."

<There is a very convenient conduit pipe leading away from engineering,> Ax said. <We had no trouble getting away. Though a few more seconds' time would not have been resented.>

"Yeah, you don't want to be in engineering right now," I said. I fought a desire to sit down. No time to rest. No time to show them how I felt. "Erek stayed in engineering?"

<He'll be safe,> Tobias said. <It would take a full-power, sustained Dracon blast to hurt him.>

"What happened on the ground?" Cassie asked.

"I don't know if Tom went after the Taxxons or not," I said evasively.

"No, I mean the men on the ground. The soldiers. James's people," Cassie clarified, knowing perfectly well that I'd deliberately misunderstood her question.

"I think we were fast enough to save most of the soldiers," I said. "James's people . . . I don't think many of them made it."

Cassie grabbed my arm. "Jake, was Rachel down there with them?"

"No."

"Then where is she? Why isn't she with us? Why won't you tell me?"

I sighed. No way to avoid it any longer. "She's with Tom." I wanted to keep my eyes on the floor.

Cassie was Rachel's best friend. Tobias, her boyfriend, if that term could apply to a hawk. I couldn't look at either of them.

"Oh, Jake . . ." Cassie cried.

<You son of a . . .> Tobias began. <You arrogant, ruthless . . . What have you done? What have you done?!>

"I can't let him get away," I said dully. "Tom's Yeerk . . . A Blade ship, probably the morphing cube? You were right, Cassie, I can't let that happen."

"Had to be," Marco said quietly. My friend Marco had seen the same necessity I had seen. He didn't like it any more than I did, but he saw the need, the inevitability.

"There has to be some other way," Cassie whispered.

<Erek will not help us gain access to the weapons systems,> Ax said. <He has degraded the helm controls so that this ship can be kept flying but cannot effectively be brought into any action. It is as if someone were trying to control the flight of the Pool ship with an oar. The Pool ship will enter orbit and not leave it until the Yeerks can perform a major system overhaul requiring many hours. The Pool ship is useless as a weapons platform, except perhaps for one or two quick shots.>

"Which we can't take because we can't access weapons controls. Our blackmail only goes so far," Marco agreed. "Erek's down to core programming, no discretion: He cannot enable a major weapons system. Flat cannot. We'll be sitting ducks if Tom turns the Blade ship against us, and we all know that's his plan."

I exploded. "It's not Tom! It's not Tom, don't call him that. It's the Yeerk in his head. It's the Yeerk, not my brother!"

No one even looked shocked at my reaction. No one was in his right mind at that moment. Tobias hated me, hated me, I could feel it, and I hated myself.

Had to be another way. I couldn't kill Rachel. Not my cousin Rachel, not after all the times she had saved my life.

"One chance and one chance only," I said. "You said it, Ax: one or two quick shots, if we had access to weapons. One or two shots, maybe we could disable the Blade ship."

"We don't have access to weapons," Marco pointed out.

I nodded. "Yeah. But Visser One does."

"Use Visser One to disable the Blade ship?" Marco frowned.

I took a couple of deep breaths. Tried to focus. There was a clock in my brain going *tick tock, tick tock,* time's up. Had to stick to the plan.

"It's time," I said. "I have to call Toby."

I began to morph tiger. I needed the morph and more importantly, I needed the thought-speak.

<Don't let her die,> Tobias said quietly. <Find a way, Jake. Don't you let her die.>

Once I was ready I called to Toby. <Toby, we're on track and on schedule. By now the bulk of available shock troops are in the engineering section, along with Visser One. Get into position: Close the engineering doors and shoot anything that tries to get out. And Toby, hold that position, no matter what. To the last person, Toby.>

"Anyone who can morph can escape that room," Cassie pointed out. "And Visser One can morph. He can get past Toby's people and take them from behind."

I nodded. <Yeah. But he won't go after Toby's people. He'll come after us because he'll know we're after his precious bridge.>

"He doesn't even know we're here," she said.

<Battle morphs, everyone. Let's inform Visser One of our presence.>

CHAPTER 22

We blew out of that room and tore down the corridor, heading directly away from engineering.

Heading, in fact, for the pool itself.

After all the pent-up watching and waiting it was good to have claws and teeth and enemies to face.

From time to time as we went, lone Hork-Bajir- or human-Controllers spotted us. Most ran and survived. Others did not run. A small patrol of what had to be some sort of Yeerk military police stood and did battle with us. They slowed us for only a few seconds.

We were moving almost too easily, encountering almost too little resistance. Visser One had to learn of our presence. He had to rush from the battle in engineering to confront a greater threat.

There were guards at the entrance to the pool itself, a pair of Hork-Bajir talking nervously about the distant firefight in engineering.

I was on the first one before he could yell. I carried him down with the momentum of my leap and slapped him with the kind of blow that only a tiger can deliver.

Ax took out the other guard and, all at once, we were in the holy of holys, the pool itself. It was perfectly round, dimly lit, under a low ceiling. It was a gray steel swimming pool lined with cages where uncooperative host bodies were kept while their Yeerks soaked up nutrients. The cages held maybe twenty or twenty-five humans and Hork-Bajir, all temporarily Yeerk-free.

I hadn't considered the possibility of freeing hosts. <Marco! The cages!>

<On it, man,> he said happily.

A Hork-Bajir voice cried, "Andalite!"

A gaggle of unprepared human-Controllers began to charge at us, drawing Dracon weapons but afraid of firing here in the sanctuary.

We blew through them before they could make up their minds. A pair of Taxxons, evidently not members of Arbron's group, came slithering out to do battle. Cassie and Tobias tore one up badly enough that his brother would finish him off.

More Hork-Bajir. A slashing, close-in battle, and we were away again.

Now the word would reach Visser One. I hoped. Hoped. He had to come to the bridge. If he stayed in engineering he would turn the tide of battle against Toby's people.

Ax said, <Prince Jake! Inside that booth, those must be controls for the pool.>

<Yeah?> I didn't get it.

<They must occasionally repair the pool itself,> Ax said. <That would mean draining it.>

<Let's go!>

A bonus. Another new element. Was that a good thing or a bad thing?

Good. Good. Maybe. I knew the way the plan played out, knew what would happen. Rachel. Tom. Inevitable.

Maybe new elements, maybe the freed prisoners, maybe this new opening, maybe the inevitable need not occur.

Maybe we could save her.

The booth Ax had spotted looked absurdly like a toll-collector's booth on the highway. It was clear plastic and perched just above the pool, jutting slightly out. There was a single Hork-Bajir inside. There were eight Hork-Bajir outside, un-

armed but ready for trouble, ready to stand and fight.

No time to think, attack!

Ax and I raced straight at them. I slashed and opened my nearest foe from belly to neck. Ax's tail whipped. Cassie came bounding up behind us and launched herself into the battle.

But the area was too narrow, we were hemmed in. Like being shoved down inside a blender set on puree. The Hork-Bajir were all around us, beating us down, slashing, cutting, pounding, tearing at us with their clawed feet.

No way to get free! I couldn't strike without hitting Ax who was shoved hard against me.

And then, on my back, snarling but helpless, I saw a Hork-Bajir leap high over my head and land like a mosh-pit surfer on my tormentors.

The prisoners! One of the Hork-Bajir prisoners Marco had released.

Marco was there now, too, but most of all, it was the freed prisoners. They turned the tide, attacking their tormentors with awesome rage.

Ax was on his hooves again, bloody, hurt, but well enough to swing his tail and cut the lock to the control booth.

A gorilla yanked the door open and said, <Hi, there! You want to live? Then lie down right now!> He grabbed the unresisting Hork-Bajir and threw him out into the fracas.

Then Marco held the door open like a hotel doorman and grinned a rubbery gorilla grin.

<Gentlemen?>

Ax pushed past me, began punching at active screens and arrays of controls.

<There is a flush sequence,> he said. <I have to override the safety protocols.>

He turned his stalk eyes to me even as his main eyes guided swift, nimble fingers.

<It can be done.>

<Okay,> I said.

<The pool is full to capacity. These are the Yeerks that were rescued from the earth-based Yeerk pool. Plus the bulk of the unhosted Yeerks recently transported here.>

<Some reason you're telling me all this, Axman?>

<Jake, there are seventeen thousand, three hundred seventy-two Yeerks in this pool.>

That rocked me.

Visser One had to know we were here, on the loose. He had to run for the bridge and not stay to win the fight in engineering.

Seventeen thousand. Living creatures. Thinking creatures. How could I give this order? Even for victory. Even to save Rachel. How could I give this kind of order?

They could have stayed home, I thought. *No*

151

one had asked them to come to Earth. Not my fault. Not my fault, theirs.

No more than they deserved.

Aliens. Parasites. Subhuman.

<Flush them,> I said.

CHAPTER 23

The Pool ship's main pool went through its standard cleaning cycle, draining the gray, sludgy water out into the vacuum of space.

The water, and the parasite creatures within it, froze instantly. The pool became an ice cloud falling away from the slow-moving Pool ship.

How many had Ax said? Seventeen thousand and . . . how many? How many Yeerks had felt the sudden stab of terror as they realized what was happening?

Frozen now. Crystals. An orbiting graveyard.

<Let's go,> I said.

We ran from that place, ran from thoughts of what we'd done. Ran for the bridge. His fault, it was Visser One's fault, all of it. Who had started this war? Not us. We hadn't asked for it.

It was him. Him and his filthy, subhuman, parasitic race.

His fault. Not mine. Not mine.

He was on the bridge when we got there, our old enemy. Visser One and a handful of Controllers, human and Hork-Bajir. But he seemed almost alone.

The main view screen showed a cloud of sparkling ice shards.

Visser One watched it, almost oblivious to us, though he surely knew we were there. Finally, he turned, and looked at me with all four of his Andalite eyes.

<So,> he said almost softly, <still not dead.>

<No, Visser. Not quite dead.>

<You're the one called Jake, aren't you? The brother of my security chief's host body.>

<That's me.>

He nodded slightly. He motioned toward the view screen as the picture changed. <As you see, my Blade ship is approaching.>

<I don't think they'll be much help to you, Visser.>

<No. It took me a while to see what had happened. But I see it now. The Blade ship will attack, and I am helpless, unable to control this ship.> He laughed mirthlessly. <Only a traitor

could have beaten me. I was not beaten by you, human, or by your pet Andalite there. I was undone by my trusting nature.>

Marco laughed then stopped himself.

<Only another Yeerk could have beaten me, and then only by the lowest treason. I was not beaten by you. Never by you.>

<Visser, you can still get off one or two shots at the Blade ship. Take out his engines.>

<Yes, we will try that very thing,> he said dryly. <But you see, someone is bleeding power out of the Dracon beams. Power is being diverted. One of the traitors at work, I suppose. We will get off one or two shots, but at one-quarter strength. Will they be enough? Unlikely.>

<Erek!> I raged in private thought-speak. <Stop draining power from the Dracon beams!>

No answer of course.

<Erek, I know you think you're doing the right thing, but you're making it worse!>

Visser One sighed. <My one consolation is that when the traitor murders me with my own ship, it will at least finally be the end of you!>

"Targeting the Blade ship's starboard engine. We are ready to fire," one of the humans reported.

Visser One waved a lazy hand. <Fire.>

On the screen I saw the beam reach out through space. Once. Twice. Both missed.

The Blade ship reacted swiftly to avoid the slow retargeting of the Pool ship's big Dracon cannon.

The Blade ship fired. The explosion reverberated through the ship.

"Engine number one is destroyed, Visser."

The Blade ship fired again. Again.

Two more explosions.

"We are without propulsion, Visser."

<Yes. I noticed that,> Visser One said. <No engines. And all our brothers in the pool murdered by these humans.>

"We are being hailed."

<Of course,> Visser One muttered. <By all means. We must play it out.>

It was Tom's face that appeared on the screen. And Tom's voice that spoke. But the smug, hard, derisive tone was that of a Yeerk.

"You seem to be experiencing some engine trouble, Visser," Tom gloated.

<The Empire will track you down and kill you, you do understand that, I hope?>

"Oh, I doubt it. I think the Empire will have its hands full," Tom's Yeerk said cheerfully. "The Andalite fleet is rather close by. It's possible that I misled you on that point."

Then he caught sight of me.

His face paled. His eyes went wide. All at once, he knew.

"You're not dead!"

<I noticed the same thing,> Visser One said dryly.

Tom snapped an order to his crew. "Bring us around to target the Pool ship's bridge. Do it! Now! Now! Bring us around!"

<Jake,> Tobias said, pleading, knowing, but pleading anyway.

<Rachel . . .> I said. <Go.>

#54 The Beginning

I was a flea on Tom's head. A flea can't see much really, just an impression of light or dark. Not my favorite morph. But if you want to hide out, unnoticed, on a human body, you can't beat the flea. And with practice you can learn to understand speech from the distant, distorted vibrations that reach your quivering antennae.

My time was coming, and I had to find a place to demorph and remorph. I fired the spring-loaded legs and catapulted into the air.

It took forever for me to fall. The first time you do it it scares the pee out of you. Falling and falling like that. Like you jumped off the moon and were falling to Earth.

I hit the deck, a fall of thousands of times my own height. Flea didn't care. Not even a bruise.

A strained voice said, "That's . . . that's not a

waste dump. They aren't dumping waste! That's the pool. The main pool. It's been flushed."

There was an audible gasp from several voices. The human-Controllers and Hork-Bajir-Controllers who were Tom's bridge crew.

"Sensors showing . . . it's our people. Sixteen thousand . . . maybe seventeen thousand."

Tom cut in harshly. "It saves us the trouble of killing them ourselves." Then, in an undertone, "But why? Why would the Visser flush . . . what does this mean?"

It means Jake's alive, Tommy Boy. You'll figure it out in a minute, Yeerk. But I'm guessing it will be too late.

Away from blood. That's where I had to go. The flea's senses were all attuned for the warm scent of blood. But that scent represented danger to me now, and I hopped away, each bounding leap the equivalent of a human jumping over the Grand Canyon. Try getting a flea morph to move *away* from blood. Amazing how much resistance you can get from a brain that's about ten cells big.

I felt shade. Absence of light. Distance from vibration. No scent of blood.

Was I in a safe place? Surely not, but maybe safe enough.

I began a slow, cautious demorph.

I heard a yell.

"The Pool ship is preparing to fire!"

"Hard left!" Tom yelled.

A moment later, Tom laughed. "The Visser's lost maneuvering ability. The Pool ship handles like a drunken Gedd at the best of times, now look at it."

Someone else reported, "His Dracon cannon is powering down. I show his reserves at less than ten percent."

"Are they? Well, well," Tom said. "Hail the visser. On screen."

I was halfway demorphed. I was a hideous creature made up of armored plates and prickly legs and human flesh spreading across me like a wave. The sickest imagination could not conjure up the true creepiness of a half-flea human. Human eyes, my own eyes, bulged from an insect face.

I could see. Not well, confused, distorted, my visual cortex still more flea than human. I was still on the bridge of the Blade ship. I was actually crouched beneath an unoccupied control station. It was like hiding under a desk. Fortunately it was designed for a Hork-Bajir body, so there was some room.

I saw the view screen light up. I saw Visser One's Andalite face. It was different. There was a dull look in his usually aggressive eyes, a slackness in the normally tensed body.

"You seem to be experiencing some engine trouble, Visser," Tom gloated.

I was completely demorphed now. There would be no room for me to morph all the way to grizzly and stay concealed. Every eye on the bridge was watching the screen, but a seven-foot bear looming up will definitely attract attention.

I started the morph. If it turned out I wasn't needed, well, then it would be fatally stupid of me. But I had no real doubt.

Visser One said, <The Empire will track you down and kill you, you do understand that, I hope?>

"Oh, I doubt it. I think the Empire will have its hands full," Tom said cheerfully. "The Andalite fleet is rather close by. It's possible that I misled you on that point."

He was all but giggling.

Then, the viewscreen widened out and he saw, and I saw, the lithe Bengal tiger standing near the visser.

Tobias was there, too.

Tom saw the tiger and knew it was Jake and knew in that split second that he had been outmaneuvered, outfought. He took a step back, like he'd been punched. "You're not dead!" he cried.

<I noticed the same thing,> Visser One said dryly.

Tom yelled, "Bring us around to target the Pool ship's bridge. Do it! Now! Now! Bring us around!"

At that moment I could have morphed all the way to elephant without being noticed. Tom's panic was infectious. They all knew they'd been had.

But they didn't know how. Tom's reaction was pure instinct: Shoot. He'd forgotten that the Pool ship was helpless. The sight of Jake, who should have been dead, standing there with the other Animorphs, standing there alive and apparently in control of the Pool ship . . . all Tom could think of was shooting.

The danger was closer than that.

Jake looked at me. Like he knew I was watching him.

<Rachel,> he said. <Go.>

<Rachel . . .> Tobias said.

<I know,> I said.

I was still not completely morphed when someone shrieked, "Animorph!"

After all these years of the Yeerks thinking we were Andalites, always yelling "Andalite!" whenever they saw a morph. It was strangely gratifying that they at last knew who we were.

I said, <That's right, genius: Animorph.>

I did what I do better than anyone. What Jake counted on me to do.

I attacked. . . .

Get into
the mind of
K.A. Applegate

Visit
www.scholastic.com/kaapplegate

Learn everything you
need to know about
Animorphs® and *Everworld*™,
and get a sneak peek
at K.A. Applegate's
new series, REMNANTS™,
in bookstores
June 2001.